'I'm on my way to bed now,' Blair told her quietly. 'I like to see that my patients are all behaving themselves before I turn in. It beats being called out just as I drift into sleep.'

'Well, I'm behaving myself,' Cari said bitterly. 'I don't think I have a choice.'

Blair grinned. 'Neither you have,' he agreed. 'And your obs are nicely settled. I can leave you with a quiet mind.'

'I'd hate to cause you a sleepless night,' Cari said harshly.

For a long moment he stayed looking down at the battered face of the girl on the pillow.

'I'll just bet you would,' he said softly. Then he turned and was gone.

Marion Lennox has had a variety of careers—medical receptionist, computer programmer and teacher. Married, with two young children, she now lives in rural Victoria, Australia. Her wish for an occupation which would allow her to remain at home with her children, her dog and the budgie led her to attempt writing a novel.

Previous titles

A BITTER JUDGEMENT
DOCTOR TRANSFORMED
CRUEL COUNTRY

WINGS OF HEALING

BY

MARION LENNOX

First published in Great Britain 1997
by Mills & Boon Limited

© Marion Lennox 1997

Australian copyright 1997
New Zealand copyright 1997
Philippine copyright 1997

ISBN 0 263 80334 8

MILLS & BOON LIMITED
ETON HOUSE   18–24 PARADISE ROAD
RICHMOND   SURREY   TW9 1SR

*First published in Great Britain 1991
by Mills & Boon Limited*

© Marion Lennox 1991

*Australian copyright 1991
Philippine copyright 1992
This edition 1992*

ISBN 0 263 77564 X

*Set in 10 on 11½ pt Linotron Times
03-9202-53716
Typeset in Great Britain by Centracet, Cambridge
Made and printed in Great Britain*

CHAPTER ONE

THE sign sixty kilometres back had been explicit. 'Aboriginal Land. No Camping Without Authority.'

Dr Cari Eliss looked at the map spread on the seat beside her and bit her lip. The area she was in was ringed with red, and emblazoned with the same warning she had seen on the sign.

Slatey Creek was still a hundred and fifty kilometres ahead, down the sandy road stretching endlessly in front of Cari's four-wheel-drive truck. According to the map, she had fifty of those kilometres to cross before she was off Aboriginal land.

She shouldn't have tried to go so far, she told herself wearily. For the last two nights she had camped on the side of the road. The thought of a settlement and a hot shower at Slatey Creek had driven her to try to cover too great a distance.

The dusk was starting to settle over the barren country, fading the brilliant reds to rusty ochres. The warnings of the locals back at Alice Springs ran in Cari's ears.

'If you've got any sense, girl, you'll be well off the road by dark. The desert may look empty, but, once night falls, the kangaroos are out in force. They don't give you any warning when they decide they want to cross the road. They can make a fair mess of themselves, of your truck and of you.'

Cari looked nervously out of her side window. Already the ground was in shadow and it was impossible to make out whether the vague shapes were blackboys—the stumpy plants that grew prolifically in this area—or kangaroos ready to spring.

The thought of Slatey Creek, with its running water and other human beings, faded in the face of Cari's nervousness. There was no choice. She was going to have to spend another night on her own.

Here. Despite the signs, she was going no further tonight. She sent a silent prayer that she wasn't desecrating any sacred site, pulled over to the edge of the road and stopped.

She had no real fear of offending anyone. Cari had seen two vehicles in the last three days and both of those had been near the Alice. On normal roads she would have been nervous of camping by herself, but here there was no reason for nervousness. Just loneliness.

She pushed the thought away. This had been her choice, to stay as far from people as she could until she had reached some sort of acceptance, some sort of decision. It was weakness to admit to needing company.

Swiftly she set to work, pitching her tent and boiling her billy on the Primus. Once she had eaten, the depression would fade. As the water heated she rummaged in the back of the truck for what she needed to make a meal.

The soft murmur of a plane's engine in the distance made her raise her head. It was still light enough to make out the aircraft, approaching low overhead. As it neared her and the murmur grew to a roar, it swooped low as if trying to make out what was disturbing the monotony of this deserted stretch of road.

Cari looked up and glared. She didn't want to be gazed on from above. As she did she caught the insignia emblazoned on the side of the plane. A pair of wings. The insignia of the Australian Flying Doctor Service.

The plane passed so low that Cari could feel a rush of wind. She put her hands to her ears to block out the deafening noise. As the plane swept over and away she breathed a sigh of relief, a relief that was shortlived. The plane went forward a few hundred metres, banked, turned and then came in low over the road alongside her campsite.

On the first run it didn't land, and for a couple of moments Cari thought that the plane had just been coming in for a closer look at her camp. Even as she thought it, she realised she was wrong. The pilot had been doing a check on the road surface. At the end of the run he banked again, turned and came in to land.

Cari groaned audibly and then, as the funny side of the situation struck her, she grinned wryly to herself. Half an hour ago she had been longing for company. Now company was dropping unexpectedly from the heavens and she was cursing!

Her amusement faded and she grimaced. She was hardly in a fit state to be seen by civilised company. She hadn't seen running water for three days. Her slim figure was clad in a grubby check shirt and torn jeans and her normally luxuriant mass of blonde hair was roughly tied back with a piece of frayed ribbon. She put a hand up to her face, and grimaced again as she did so. Her hand was blackened from the frypan she had just pulled from the truck, and she knew that now she would have endowed herself with a streak of black across her face.

Why had they stopped? She thought briefly of the signs she had ignored and rejected the idea. The Flying Doctor was hardly likely to take law enforcement as one of its tasks. As the plane taxied to a halt she stayed where she was, watching and waiting.

The pilot brought the plane to within metres of her truck. As she watched, the rear door opened and a man dropped down easily on to the road surface. Behind him in the open doorway, a girl dressed in nurse's uniform watched curiously.

The man who emerged stopped for a moment before coming towards Cari, taking his time in absorbing the scene in front of him. He was in his mid-thirties, Cari guessed, lean, superbly muscled and tall, much taller than Cari. He was casually attired in light trousers and open-necked shirt. His eyes were permanently creased as if to ward off this too harsh sun. His dark brown hair was bleached fair where it grew longer as if it too had seen too much sun.

His bearing spoke of authority and professionalism. Cari nodded to herself as she acknowledged his intro-duction. She had been right in her guess as to his occupation.

'I'm Dr Blair Kinnane.'

He was carefully appraising the slight girl in front of him. She looked exhausted, he thought dispassionately, with heavy shadows around her big green eyes. He could see no sign of injury or illness, though.

'Are you all right?' His voice, when he spoke, was deeply resonant.

'Yes,' Cari replied slowly. She looked up at the man in front of her with a puzzled frown.

'You're not injured?'

'No.'

'Is your vehicle OK?'

'Yes.'

Blair Kinnane let his breath out in a sigh of pure exasperation.

'Then would you mind telling me what the hell you're doing camped on Kinjarra land?'

'Kinjarra. . .' Cari was lost.

'Kinjarra land.' Dr Kinnane motioned around him with a sweeping gesture. 'All around here is owned by the Kinjarra tribe. Now unless I miss my bet you, sweetheart, are an American.' His voice was low with anger. 'You don't belong to any Aboriginal group that I know of, and I'm willing to place bets that you don't have permission to camp on their land. Do you?' he demanded savagely.

'I. . . No.'

He closed his eyes wearily. 'Our pilot has just put at risk the lives of all the people on board this plane by landing at dusk on an unknown road. Do you know why he did that?'

'N-No.' Cari was off balance and confused.

'Because we thought there was something wrong,' Dr Kinnane went on roughly. 'People don't camp in this area. It's country where there's no fresh water for miles and there are signs up on all the maps forbidding camping. It was natural for us to assume you were in trouble.' He gestured towards the plane. 'I've got a sick child in there. I hope you're proud of yourself!'

Cari was pale with distress. 'I'm so sorry,' she managed to say. 'I didn't think——'

'No,' he cut her short, 'your kind never do.' He glanced at his watch. 'You've got three minutes to pack up your gear and get out of here.'

'But. . .' Cari was horrified, 'I can't just leave!'

'Why not?' The doctor's tone had assumed a level of supreme uninterest. Behind him Cari caught the expression of the nurse and the pilot still in the plane. They were obviously deriving considerable amusement from her discomfiture.

'Because it's dusk.' Cari stared up at Blair Kinnane's implacable face as she spoke. Deep within, a bubble of anger stirred. 'I've been told these roads are dangerous to travel on by night.'

'So why did you enter Aboriginal land when you knew you couldn't reach the other side before dark?'

'I thought the roads would be better than they have been,' Cari said defensively. 'I had to slow down to a crawl for about twenty kilometres because of sand that's drifted across. I was planning to be at Slatey Creek by now.'

He nodded. 'And you're not.' He motioned politely towards the tent. 'Nevertheless, you can't stay here.'

'Why not?' Cari demanded angrily. 'I'm not disturbing anything. I'm damned if I'm going to risk my life by driving in these conditions. No Aboriginal is going to come here and hunt me off!'

'No,' Blair agreed, 'they're not. The Kinjarra are a gentle, self-effacing people who would never dream of demanding that you leave.'

'So why should I?'

'Because you're disturbing their land.' He spoke patiently, as if to a difficult child. He gestured to the surrounding countryside. 'The people here are dependent on this land for their sustenance. They've chosen to live the way their people have for thousands of years. They depend on the wildlife here for food. It's enough that they've allowed a road through their land. If camping was allowed the wildlife would be driven further and further back. There have to be areas where the only people to exist are the Kinjarra, otherwise their tribal way of life hasn't a hope of continuing.'

Cari glared at the man in front of her. She was tired and she was hungry. This man, with his implacable logic, was going to force her to keep driving on this awful road. To her horror she felt tears well in her eyes. She turned away abruptly and started throwing her cooking implements back into the truck.

'If you're worried about driving,' Blair Kinnane's voice continued, and by its softening Cari knew that he'd seen the tears, 'you could leave your truck here and come in to Slatey Creek with us.'

For a crazy moment the logic was appealing. To have someone else transport her the last kilometres. . .

'But the truck. . .' she began.

'You'd have to get someone to drive you out here tomorrow and bring it in. It'd cost you a bit,' Blair said reflectively. With anger Cari heard the touch of amusement in his voice. He obviously had her pegged as a 'rich bitch'.

'Never mind,' she said tightly. 'Thank you for your offer, but I'll look after myself.' She bent down and started pulling tent pegs from the soft, sandy soil.

For a moment Blair stood looking down at the seemingly frail figure at his feet. Despite himself he was intrigued by this wisp of a girl with her fierce independence and stubborn pride. What on earth was she doing in such an area as this? He shook his head.

'Are you sure you can manage?'

Cari didn't look up. 'Quite sure,' she said bitterly. 'You don't have to stay and watch. You have my word that I'll get out of here.'

'Are you right to go, Blair?' It was the nurse, an attractive girl of about Cari's age, her voice full of soft amusement, approaching to stand at Blair's side. 'We do have a patient,' she reminded him humorously. 'Much as we'd love to stay and chat.' The last words were directed at Cari's bent back, and Cari flashed her a look of venom before resuming her task.

'OK, Liz.' Blair looked at the girl kneeling with her

back turned to him. 'You'd be best advised to take us up on the offer of a lift,' he said brusquely. 'You're obviously tired, and this country's no place to be driving through by yourself at night.'

'Thank you for your advice,' Cari said through clenched teeth. 'I don't need your help.'

Blair shrugged his shoulders. There was nothing more he could do. He motioned to the pilot. 'We're not needed here,' he called. 'Let's get home.'

Cari stayed bent over her tent pegs until the sound of the plane's engines faded into the night. Then she put her face in her hands and burst into tears of weariness, humiliation and anger.

By the time the camp had been packed away and Cari had recovered some measure of self-possession it was fully dark. She forced herself to eat a couple of biscuits from her supplies in the back. Her hunger had faded, but she knew that she had to be alert for the next few hours. Her billy had boiled on the Primus, so she made herself a couple of mugs of strong coffee before she climbed behind the wheel again.

Her anger was fading, leaving her feeling sick at herself for her behaviour. The man back there—Dr Kinnane—had been right, she acknowledged to herself. To have put the little plane down in the middle of nowhere to check on her welfare. . .

It made her feel a little less alone on this vast, uninhabited plain. The thought of Blair Kinnane's deep, angry eyes came before her and stayed insistently in her mind. He had cared, she thought sadly. No matter how much of a damned fool he thought she was, he still was concerned. It was a long time since she had met a doctor with a commitment like that.

At least the road was reasonable. Cari acknowledged

the impossibility of making Slatey Creek that night. All she intended was to reach the border of the restricted area. The thought of setting up her bleak little camp again left her cold.

Why was she doing this? Not for the first time she questioned her own sanity. She shook her head and fumbled beside her in the cassette case for some music. She would dearly have liked the company of commercial radio, but such a luxury was unheard-of in these remote parts.

She saw no kangaroos at all, and after a while she relaxed. Perhaps the warnings had been over-dramatisation. There was nothing out there but an endless horizon of barren desert. The cassette started, and the songs from a jazz concert Cari had attended years before filled the cabin. Ahead, the road stretched in a darkening ribbon and her foot crept down on the accelerator.

The roo came from nowhere. One minute the road was clear; the next Cari's vision was full of kangaroo.

Her foot dived desperately for the brake. Her hands hauled the steering-wheel, but there was nothing she could do to avoid the huge roo. The truck lurched to one side, struck and skidded into the soft sand at the side of the road. It lurched again, the road side wheels lost their hold and the truck fell sickeningly to its side.

Its momentum took it all the way over. Almost it came back up to its wheels again before gravity caught it. It settled back on to its side. The wheels of the little truck stopped spinning and it was still.

CHAPTER TWO

CARI surfaced to the sound of jazz. A familiar woman's voice was filling the night, half crooning, half singing the beautiful 'Misty'. For a moment Cari thought she was back in that concert hall of years ago, mesmerised by the glorious music. Then the pain struck.

It knifed through her legs like fire, so sharply that she cried out. There was no one to hear.

Fully conscious now, Cari tried to work out what had happened. The truck was on its side. She was still in the cabin, wedged behind the steering-wheel and hanging backwards on the seat.

It was still pitch black. She didn't know how long she had been unconscious. Moments, perhaps.

The music was still reverberating through the truck. 'Misty' finished and a big band number took over. The sound in the tiny cabin was unbearable. Cari twisted, crying out in pain as she did so, and hit the buttons of the cassette player. The music died. The silence of the desert took over.

She was caught, trapped beneath the twisted steering column. Her head was aching, a dull throb. Tentatively she put a hand to her hair, and it came away wet and sticky. Blood was oozing down her face. She could taste it, warm and salty on her tongue.

She couldn't stay in here. Frantically she pushed the steering column, trying to shove it from her body, but it was immovable. She seized it again and hauled herself up. Despite the shards of pain she pulled with all her strength, trying to get her pelvis free. It moved,

14

a fraction of movement that made her pull harder. The pain caught and held, shock upon shock of agonising sensation.

It was too much. The dullness in her head stirred and whirled in a dizzy throbbing. The night closed in on her and, once more, Cari fell into unconsciousness.

For the next few hours she drifted in and out of consciousness. Night became day. Inside the truck the heat gradually built up as the sun gained power. The truck was providing shade but nothing else.

At one time as she surfaced into consciousness Cari groped behind her, trying desperately to reach for the water container. It was just out of her reach. There was no way she could reach the water and there was no way she could move.

Desolation and hopelessness swept over her. This was the culmination of her life, she thought bitterly. First there had been the court case and the end of her medical career, then Harvey's abandonment of her, and now this. It was too much. She might as well be dead, she told herself despairingly. In fact, she soon would be. In this heat, with no water. . .

The next few hours were a haze of heat and pain. Cari's thirst became almost unbearable. As each wave of pain reached a crescendo, oblivion mercifully engulfed her. Always she surfaced to a new level of horror. She lost track of the hours passing.

And somewhere within the horror the image of the last person she had seen, the lean, accusing form of Blair Kinnane, imposed itself and stayed. The plane she had seen the night before, with its insignia of wings of healing, became a talisman that she could hold out against her terror.

'He'll come again,' she whispered over and over to

herself. It became a silent chant of belief. 'He'll come again. He'll come.'

The drone of the aircraft started almost as background music to her chant. As it increased in volume, so did the chant in her head. It wasn't until the drone had increased to a roar as the aircraft landed and then was suddenly silent that Cari realised her chant had become reality.

Even then the waves of unconsciousness were increasing to the extent where consciousness was simply a half-state of awareness.

There was the sound of shouting and running feet. Then the back door of the truck was flung open. Cari's sight to the back of the truck was restricted to the view given by the tiny square of mirror above her head, reflecting backwards. She brought her gaze up, to meet Blair Kinnane's concerned grey eyes.

'I knew you'd come,' she said.

Cari could afterwards recollect little of the next few hours. She knew it took time to free her from the twisted wreck of the truck, but the painkillers Blair injected deepened her haze. She remembered him crawling through the back of the truck and holding water to her lips and murmuring words of reassurance. She supposed an injection must have followed.

In a sense his presence was enough. For some reason it dispelled her fears. The rest would follow. Her release was inevitable with this man in charge. Afterwards she mocked herself for her childish confidence, but at the time it was natural and entirely logical.

Finally she was out of the prison of a cabin, into the harsh and brilliant sunlight. A stretcher was waiting, and Cari recognised the same faces she had seen the night before. She remembered trying to smile acknowl-

edgment and thanks. That was all. Her plane trip to
Slatey Creek was non-existent, as was the ambulance
ride from the air-strip to the hospital. She slept.

She woke to find herself in an examination cubicle of a
hospital. For a moment, the drug-induced sleep cleared
from her head and she looked around her. It was odd
to be staring at a hospital from this angle. She had
always managed to be on the examining side of the
trolleys before this.

Blair Kinnane was at her side. He was turned away,
adjusting some instruments. He looked strong, Cari
thought drowsily. Strong and competent.

The fog of pain, shock and drugs wasn't allowing her
to think. She attempted to give herself a mental shake,
but the drugs she had been given would allow her to
do no such thing.

Blair turned back to the bed and smiled briefly at the
ashen face on the pillow.

'So you're with us, Cari?'

'How did you know my name?' Her voice was slurred
and slow.

He motioned to the desk behind him. Cari followed
his gesture and could see her travel-bag, its contents
spilled out on to the surface of the bench.

'We checked,' he smiled. 'You've been in no condition to ask.'

'I. . . What happened?'

'You hit an old man kangaroo. Don't you
remember?'

Cari thought back. 'Did I kill him?' Suddenly the
question seemed absurdly important.

Blair nodded. 'Instantly, I imagine,' he said drily.
'You very nearly did the same thing to yourself. You
must have been travelling at speed.'

There was criticism in his tone, and Cari heard it. All of a sudden the events of the last few hours overwhelmed her. She remembered all the magnificent kangaroos she had seen in the last few days, and that she had been responsible for the death of even one of these animals made her feel sick. Tears rolled down her face.

'I'm sorry,' she said brokenly. She turned her face into the pillow.

Blair looked down at the face beneath him, his face twisting curiously. 'Well, perhaps the lessons on road safety can wait,' he said curtly. He looked up to the sister at his side. 'Is Theatre ready?'

'Theatre?' The word sank into Cari's distressed mind.

'We've some repair work to do.' Blair was watching her again, his face grave.

'My pelvis is broken?' Her voice wouldn't work properly.

She wanted to know the medical details, but instead she got a layman's summary.

'Yes. We've X-rayed it and it's stable—that means we don't have to set it. You're going to be with us for a while, though, while it mends.' He put a hand down and touched her shoulder reassuringly, sensing her rising panic. 'Don't worry,' he smiled, 'we'll look after you.'

When he smiled his face lit up, forcing an almost instinctive reaction in Cari. Her eyes met his, and her panic receded. Once again the drug-induced euphoria took over. This man could do anything he liked to her, and she wouldn't care.

His smile faded. For a long moment he stood looking at the face beneath him on the pillow. Their eyes locked and held.

The door swung, and an open-faced young man entered the room. His white coat with casual clothes underneath also labelled him a doctor.

'Cari, this is Dr Rod Daniels,' said Blair, breaking his gaze with an effort. By the look of your papers he's a countryman of yours.'

Cari looked towards the newcomer, confused.

'I'm American too,' Rod Daniels smiled down at her. 'New York.'

'I'm Californian,' Cari said weakly.

He grinned. 'Well, we won't hold that against you.' He looked up at Blair. 'Ready when you are.'

'Right.' Blair had been loading an injection. He smiled down again at Cari. 'It's time for you to go to sleep.'

CHAPTER THREE

THE following days passed in a drug-induced blur. Cari was aware of Blair Kinnane's concerned face intermittently over her, his gentle fingers probing, examining. There were nurses, injections and people saying words that she couldn't follow, but little else.

Finally she surfaced. Four days after the accident she woke to brilliant sunlight streaming in over the harsh white counterpane of a hospital bed. For a moment she didn't know where she was, and then the memory of the accident came flooding back.

Her head still hurt and the light hurt her eyes. She forced them to stay open until she had examined her surroundings.

There was a saline drip above her bed, and she nodded to herself. By the time she was found she would have been badly dehydrated.

Her legs. . . It was her pelvis, she remembered. She closed her eyes and concentrated. First she moved, ever so gingerly, the toes on one foot, then the toes on the other. They worked. There was pain there, but they worked.

At least it didn't seem to be her spine. She thought back to her training. Complication of pelvic inury. Bladder. . . Had they checked it? Blair Kinnane had seemed competent, but then Cari could hardly expect skilled medical care in a place like Slatey Creek.

The door of her room opened and Blair walked in.

'Good morning,' he said gravely.

Morning. Cari looked wonderingly at the window.

'What day is it?' she asked.

'Friday.'

'I've lost four days!'

Blair smiled. 'Well, there was nothing special about Monday to Thursday. They'll be staging re-runs next week.' He picked up her chart and looked down.

'What's wrong?' He was staring at the thing too long for Cari's liking.

He replaced the chart on to its clip at the end of the bed and came up to stand beside her pillows.

'Nothing,' he reassured her. 'We've done everything right, and, so far, so have you.'

'Apart from smashing myself up in the first place.'

He smiled acknowledgment. 'As you say.'

Cari glared up at him. 'You don't have to grin,' she told him fiercely. 'I'm laying odds you're thinking I deserved everything I got.'

'Well. . .' His smile remained. With it in place he looked nice, Cari thought. Nice. . .

She smiled ruefully. 'OK,' she agreed, 'I deserved what I got.'

'Well, perhaps a spanking would have been more in order than a fractured pelvis and eighteen or so hours of being trapped as you were.'

'A spanking?' Cari gasped. 'How old do you think I am?'

'Not very old,' he said firmly. 'In wisdom if not in years.' He held up a hand to silence her involuntary protest. 'I know—according to your driver's licence you're twenty-seven years old. If you are that age,' he looked doubtfully down at the girl in the bed, 'then you're old enough to know better.'

'Thanks,' Cari said bitterly.

'Do you want to go to Perth?' he asked abruptly.

'Perth?'

Blair nodded. 'We thought of sending you straight there on Monday, but you'd lost a lot of blood and were deeply shocked and dehydrated, so it seemed more sensible to stabilise you here. Now, however, you've a long hospital stay in front of you, and you might prefer to be in a big hospital.'

'I'd fly there?'

'By air ambulance, yes,' he agreed.

Cari closed her eyes for a moment. She was still as weak as a kitten and the effort of concentration was taking its toll. Perth. Her father would be enquiring after her. The first place he'd try would be the big city hospitals. Not looking for a patient, but for a doctor. Cari Eliss. It was an unusual name. With her luck. . . She opened her eyes.

'No, thank you,' she said firmly. 'If you're happy to treat me, I'm happy to stay here.'

Blair inclined his head in acknowledgment. 'Your parents?' he asked briefly. 'They wouldn't want you to have second opinions, specialist care?'

'You really do think I'm a spoiled rich kid, don't you?' Cari said bitterly.

For answer Blair picked up the admission form which was lying on the shelf near the bed.

'Occupation?' he demanded. 'It's been left blank. Can I fill it in?'

She shook her head. 'I haven't got one,' she said. 'Now are you satisfied? It's what you wanted to hear, isn't it? Cari Eliss, wealthy, indulged American tourist doing all the wrong things and having to be rescued by the oh, so efficient Dr Blair Kinnane.'

He shook his head. 'What you've been in the past is a matter of indifference to me,' he said steadily. 'If you intend staying here, then for the next few weeks you'll be my patient. Nothing else need concern me.'

'No lectures?' Cari demanded.

He smiled perfunctorily, the smile not touching his eyes.

'No lectures,' he told her. 'In a month or so you can leave here and go on being as stupid as you like for the rest of your life. All I'm concerned about is getting your body back to the stage where it'll support you in your foolhardy endeavours. Now, let's have a look at my handiwork.'

Ten minutes later her bedclothes were back in place.

'It's all looking much better.' Blair's professional smile was in place.

'What's better?' Cari asked bitterly, closing her eyes. 'Certainly not my head.' Her voice was still slurred and she realised that her mouth was bruised and swollen.

Blair nodded sympathetically. 'It is better,' he reassured her. 'You should have seen your head when you came in! You looked like something from a late-night horror movie—after the vampire had called.'

Cari attempted to return his smile. 'I thought vampires disposed of their blood more thoughtfully.' She put a hand up to feel the dressing.

'You'll never know it's happened,' Blair reassured her. 'The gash on your leg was actually more serious.'

'And my pelvis?'

'The pelvis is broken but hasn't moved. You'll be immobile for a week and here for at least another three weeks.' He met her look of dismay and reassured her gently, 'You've been lucky.'

Cari laughed mirthlessly. 'Some wouldn't think so.'

He shook his head. 'Well, you have, and make no mistake about that. There's plenty who've done what you've done and ended up dead. And if you hadn't been found for another twenty-four hours, that's just what you'd have been.'

'OK, OK,' Cari raised a hand weakly, 'I was lucky.'

'You can say that again!' It was a nurse coming through the door behind Blair. She nodded to him. 'Mr Sanderson's drip's come out,' she said apologetically.

Blair sighed. 'Right, Maggie, I can take a hint.' He gave Cari a curt nod, turned and left.

The nurse came up to the bed and introduced herself as she started neatening Cari's bedclothes.

'I'm Matron Brompton,' she said. 'You can call me Maggie if you like—everybody else around here does.'

'I'm Cari Eliss.'

'I know,' Maggie admitted. 'I've already filled out your admission forms from your driver's licence. And you're all the way from the United States. What on earth are you doing here?'

'Just travelling,' Cari said abruptly.

'On your own?' Maggie shook her head. 'In this sort of country? You must be crazy! Or brave. Or both, I guess. Do you know much about cars?'

'Not enough to keep one on the road,' Cari smiled.

'I meant mechanically,' Maggie grinned. 'Aren't you afraid of breaking down?'

'I know enough,' said Cari.

'So what do you do when you're not travelling the world?' Maggie asked curiously.

Cari hesitated. The question was suddenly too hard to answer. 'Nothing,' she said finally. 'I don't have a job.'

Maggie looked curiously at her. 'Lucky for some,' she said. 'You must have luck on your side. For some reason you had Blair Kinnane worried enough about you to take the plane off course and check on your whereabouts. If he hadn't you'd be dead. Now, open your mouth.' She popped in the thermometer and picked up Cari's wrist.

For the moment the conversation was over. Cari tried to digest the information she had just received, but it was too much. By the time the thermometer came out, her eyes were closing. Twenty minutes or so of conversation had been all she could manage.

When next she woke the room was dimmed and Blair Kinnane was again at the end of her bed. He was studying the chart and frowning. For a moment Cari could watch his harsh features without being observed.

What sort of man was he? she wondered. The frown on his face spoke of gravity. He obviously took his job seriously. For now, she was in the hands of this outback doctor, whether she liked it or not.

Her instinct was to trust him absolutely, and she hoped her instincts weren't about to let her down. With her pelvis broken and her leg badly cut, if this man wasn't skilled she could be left with nerve damage, or worse.

She thought back to the inevitable fuss if this had happened to her in the United States. Her father was a professor of surgery. He would have had her surrounded by every specialist that he could organise. Even now, if she let him know. . .

Heaven forbid. She turned her face into the pillow at the thought of his probable reaction. Her slight movement caught Blair's attention and he turned towards her.

'Just checking,' he told her quietly. 'Go back to sleep.'

She managed a smile. She must be sleeping twenty-three out of twenty-four hours.

'Do you ever sleep yourself?' she asked drowsily. She glanced at her bedside clock. It was midnight.

'I'm on my way to bed now,' he told her. 'I like to

see that my patients are all behaving themselves before I turn in. It beats being called out just as I drift into sleep.'

'Well, I'm behaving myself,' Cari said bitterly. 'I don't think I have a choice.'

Blair grinned. 'Neither you have,' he agreed. 'And your obs are nicely settled. I can leave you with a quiet mind.'

'I'd hate to cause you a sleepless night,' she said harshly.

For a long moment he stayed looking down at the battered face of the girl on the pillow.

'I'll just bet you would,' he said softly. Then he turned and was gone.

It was another week before Cari's world assumed anything like its normal course. Slowly, however, her level of painkilling drugs could be reduced. The shock, the bruising and the swelling reduced to a point where she could take some notice of her surroundings and the people who were caring for her.

Her relationship with Dr Kinnane remained curt and strained. She had a solid impression that he disapproved of her, and would have been very happy to see her on a plane to Perth. Ignoring his repeated suggestions, she stayed where she was. Perth held no appeal. Slatey Creek held little either, but at least she was safe from her family's enquiries.

The hospital was busy. It had twenty beds and the turnover seemed to be rapid. Cari was in a two-bed ward, and the occupant in the next bed seemed continuously to be changing.

Cari soon learned to know the hospital staff. With Maggie she achieved an instant rapport, and she also struck up an easy friendship with Dr Rod Daniels.

More and more he was drawn to Cari's bedside. Cari intrigued him. As the swelling and bruising from the accident subsided, he was seeing and appreciating her blossoming beauty. Even the hospital issue nightwear and a dressing over one side of her face couldn't disguise it.

'What part of California are you from?' he asked.

'I'd rather not talk about my home, Dr Daniels.' Cari followed her words with a smile and the words were robbed of offence. She wasn't going to be drawn into a discussion of her background.

Rod took the snub with good humour. Cari continued to intrigue him. It was obvious she was reluctant to discuss her background, but her very reluctance made her more interesting.

'So why are *you* here?' she asked him, directing the topic of conversation away from herself.

'I'm here for the excitement,' he said morosely, and then, as Cari's face queried him, he continued, 'I've always had a vision of the Flying Doctor Service being the most exciting job a medico could hold.' He held out his hands expressively. 'So what happens? I sign up for two years, they put me behind a radio set and I spend my time doing exactly what I'd be doing in general practice, with the added problem that half the time I haven't got a patient to look at. I only get to hear the symptoms.'

'I imagine in some cases that might be an advantage,' Cari said drily. She eased herself in the bed, trying to find a comfortable position.

'Still bad?' Rod asked sympathetically. He picked up her chart. 'I can order something if you like.'

Cari shook her head. 'No, thanks. Blair's already offered, but I've had enough. For here on in I'm putting up with a bit of discomfort. At least my head's my own that way.'

Rod went on his way, and Cari settled back to sleep. It was visiting hours, and the woman in the next bed was surrounded by family and friends. Until now Cari had been too ill to mind, drifting in and out of sleep as her body recovered. Now. . . Sleep wouldn't come.

For the first time she faced the thought of the future. Soon she would be able to try to stand and move about the hospital. If she had somewhere to go, in another couple of weeks she could go home. Not to drive, though. It would be weeks—months even—before she could contemplate travelling by herself again. She guessed she could fly back to Perth once she was out of hospital. Slatey Creek was hardly the place for recuperating. Perth. . .

It was going to cost money. Her limited funds were all but dried up. She had insurance on the truck, but how long that would take to come through she didn't know. And she had her return ticket to the States.

She couldn't go home yet. She couldn't. She wasn't ready to face her family, her friends with their easy sympathy.

What could she do? For years now medicine had been her whole life. Medicine and Harvey. Without them she seemed a shell, a ghost of her former self.

'Tears, Cari?'

It was Blair. The man moved like a cat, Cari thought, reaching desperately for a handkerchief.

'Are you in pain?' His deep eyes were assessing.

'No.' It was nearly true.

There was a long moment of silence. Cari blew her nose and looked up defiantly. 'I'm fine, thank you, Dr Kinnane.'

He nodded. 'Just suffering a case of the doldrums?'

He looked at her closely. 'Cari, what's your reason for not permitting us to contact your family? Surely you have someone who'll be worried about you?'

Worried! Cari had to suppress a bitter laugh. Her family would be worried all right. They'd be worried at what else she could possibly be doing to disgrace the family name, shaming the great Professor Eliss and his successful sons. She thought suddenly of her mother. Her mother would be worried, she thought, and for Cari's sake. She wouldn't be admitting it to her husband, though.

Cari sighed and shook her head. 'I'm on my own,' she said firmly.

'A lady of independent means,' Blair remarked lightly.

'I don't know about means,' Cari said bitterly. 'But yes, I'm certainly independent.'

His eyes narrowed. 'Are you in trouble financially?' he asked bluntly.

'No.'

'No?'

She looked up to meet his eyes. Why did he make her feel like an errant schoolgirl? An errant schoolgirl with a crush. . .

'My financial affairs are none of your business,' she retorted brusquely. 'Now, if you don't mind, can you just do what you came to do and leave me alone?'

It was ungracious and ungrateful, but the words were all she could manage. Why did this man make her feel more than ever like turning into her pillow and wallowing in self-pity?

She did just that. As Blair finished his brief examination and left her to it she buried her head and wallowed.

Five minutes later she was interrupted again.

'What's this? Tears?'

It was Maggie, bearing a steaming cup of hot chocolate.

Cari managed a watery smile and pushed herself into a half-sitting position. She took the cup gratefully.

'Since when has it become the matron's job to deliver supper?'

'This isn't supper. It's not official.' Maggie motioned to the screen behind which the patient in the next bed was entertaining visitors. 'Every patient in the hospital has a roomful, except you. And Dr Kinnane seemed to think you could use a shoulder to cry on.'

She pulled up a chair and eyed Cari shrewdly. 'Sometimes a girl needs another woman, no matter how sympathetic her doctor is.'

'Blair Kinnane is not sympathetic,' Cari sniffed.

Maggie looked at her shrewdly. 'You'd be surprised,' she said drily. 'Now, would you like to spill a few problems?'

'I. . . I don't. . .'

'Like, what are you going to do when you get out of here?' Maggie demanded.

'I don't know. . . I haven't thought,' Cari admitted.

'Will you go back to Perth?'

'I might have to wait until I get the money from my truck,' Cari confessed. 'Contrary to Dr Kinnane's opinion, I'm actually tight for money.'

Maggie frowned. 'How have you been supporting yourself?'

'I've been doing casual work as I've been travelling,' Cari explained. 'Waitressing, cleaning—anything I could get, really. Just so I could have enough to extend my stay here.'

'And why do you want to do that?'

'Because I don't want to go home.' It was out before she could stop herself.

'Why not?' The question was blunt and firm. Cari looked up at Maggie's kindly eyes and then down again, into the remnants of her hot chocolate.

'Because there are things at home I can't face yet,' she said simply.

'People?'

'And situations.'

There was a drawn-out silence. For a moment Cari thought Maggie would question her further, but, even as she thought it, she realised that this kindly woman would do no such thing. Instead, she took the mug from Cari and stood up.

'If you're worried about where to stay until you're fit, I can help,' she offered. 'Jock, my husband, manages the Slatey Creek station. We've got a big, ramshackle old house about four kilometres from town. If you can put up with two small boys, assorted livestock and heaps of dust, you're more than welcome to stay.'

Cari looked up, startled. 'I. . . It's lovely of you to offer, but I wouldn't want to put you. . .'

'To any bother.' Maggie finished for her. She grinned. 'You wouldn't. I save the efficient, hard-working me for the hospital. At home it's every man for himself. And frankly, we'd all love the company. Visitors are something we don't get much of around here.'

Cari smiled. 'Well, if you're sure.' She felt as if a huge weight had been lifted from her mind.

'I'm sure.' Maggie looked down at the too pale face on the pillows. She put a hand out and touched Cari's matted hair. 'Tell you what,' she said cheerfully, 'why don't I fetch a bowl of water and have a shot at cleaning your hair?'

Cari touched her head ruefully. 'I was thinking of chopping it all off,' she confessed. Until now she had been too ill to think of it very much at all, and the effort of trying to clean and unknot the tangle was beyond her.

'It'd be a shame,' Maggie said. She touched it again. 'From what I can see under the mess it's in, it must be lovely.'

An hour later Cari was exhausted but clean. Her hair was back to the shiny golden mane it had been in the past. She lay back, her hair framing her face in a soft cloud.

'There!' Maggie exclaimed, packing away the little blow-dryer. She smiled. 'I'm about a mile behind in the list of things I had to do tonight, but it was worth it. Don't you agree?'

Cari moved her head blissfully, enoying the softness of the newly cleaned hair.

'Lovely,' she said gratefully. Sleep was rapidly over-coming her, but she forced her eyes wide and looked directly at Maggie. 'I'm very grateful,' she said softly.

Maggie stood up. 'If you weren't, I wouldn't do it,' she laughed. She put her hand down and touched the soft hair. 'Boy, I'd kill for hair like that.' She touched her neat dark bun ruefully. 'Or rather Jock would. He fantasises about hair like yours.'

'So why did he marry you? He can't be all that taken with blondes.'

'I'm good in bed,' Maggie grinned. 'Also his mum told him I had great childbearing hips.'

Cari laughed, and snuggled into her pillow. Despite her problems and Blair Kinnane's censorious attitude, tonight she would sleep.

She was on the edge of consciousness, drifting into a deep sleep, when Blair Kinnane did his final check.

The ward was in semi-darkness. Cari sensed his presence but was too tired to acknowledge him.

She was expecting him to speak, examine her chart, or start the formalities of a visit. It didn't happen. For a long time he stayed at the side of the bed, looking down at the pale oval face surrounded by a mist of hair.

For a while Cari watched him through half-closed eyes, then the effort became too much. In a haze of contentment, she drifted off to sleep.

CHAPTER FOUR

CARI woke to the same sense of wellbeing. The pain was fading. The bruising was subsiding and she was gloriously clean. Her hair moved with her as she stirred. The early morning sun was streaming in the window, casting a filtered pattern on the white counterpane.

Cari lay motionless, trying to work out why she felt this lightness within her. It was a feeling that hadn't been there for a year now.

The vision of Blair Kinnane suddenly came into her mind. His face watching her last night, quietly watching over her as she faded into sleep. . .

She shook her head involuntarily, rejecting the idea. It was Maggie's kindness, she told herself sharply. She had found a friend.

She would take her up on her offer of accommodation, she thought. It would be fun to stay on an outback station, and she was sure she could make herself useful.

Another month's grace, she thought gratefully. Another month before decisions had to be made.

The hospital was stirring. Soon Cari's quiet reflections were disturbed as she was washed, her bed was changed and breakfasts were brought round.

She had just finished eating when Blair appeared. He smiled at her as he walked in the door and her heart gave an unfamiliar lurch. What was it about this man? she asked herself crossly.

'How are you this morning?' he asked her formally.

'Fine.' She pushed to the back of her mind the persistent image of him standing over her the night before. Surely it had been a figment of her imagination, the dream of someone who was alone in the world and needed. . .

Needed what? She flinched inwardly. There was nothing she needed, she chided herself. Nothing and no one.

He picked up the chart from the base of the bed and nodded. 'You're doing well. I think it's time this morning to see if you can cope with the walking-frame.'

Cari nodded. 'I'd like that,' she said. 'The sooner I can get mobile the better.' She smiled up at him. 'It's not that I don't appreciate your hospital,' she told him.

'I know.' He returned the smile. 'Home's better. Do you want us to organise a flight to Perth for you when you get out of here?'

Cari's smile faded. Once again she had the feeling that this man wanted her gone, the sooner the better.

'You aren't getting rid of me even then,' she told him. 'Matron has offered me a place to stay until I'm fit to drive again.'

He sighed and nodded grimly. 'I might have known!'

She met his look. 'Might have known?' she echoed.

'Matron has a soft heart.'

'You sound like you disapprove.'

He raised his eyebrows. 'Did I say that?'

Cari gritted her teeth. 'You didn't have to,' she muttered.

He looked at her consideringly. 'No,' he said after a moment. 'I didn't have to. Now, if you'll excuse me. . .' He turned and left. Cari glared at his retreating back. For all the world she felt like poking her tongue out.

Maggie wasn't on duty, and Cari missed her cheerful

presence. When Maggie was off duty, Liz McKinley was in charge. Liz was the sister who had been on the plane with Blair. In contrast to Maggie's warm humour, Liz was coolly efficient. When she was on duty there was no friendly chatter, and any other of the nurses who paused to talk to Cari were soon reminded of their duties.

Liz was young, attractive and vivacious. It hadn't taken Cari long lying in her bed and listening to the gossip going on around her to realise that Liz McKinley's ambitions centred firmly on Blair Kinnane.

She learned a lot from just listening. Even though her horizons were bounded by the bed, she soon had a fair idea of what was going on in the rest of the hospital.

The radio was its nerve centre. Though she couldn't see it, Cari could imagine the constantly manned machine. There were normal clinics via radio, she gathered, but, as well as that, most urgent calls or patients on their way in were pre-empted by a radio call. Cari listened and learned. The tone of the operator as he summoned Blair or Dr Daniels told how urgent the call was.

Either Blair or Rod tried to be always available. Many of the urgent calls needed immediate medical advice, and it wasn't always possible.

There were clinics to be done at the outlying settlements. This morning Cari lay and listened to Blair and one of the nurses checking their equipment. The settlement they were visiting was a hundred kilometres east, and Cari gathered that the roads were practically non-existent. They would have to use the plane. After they left, Rod was in charge.

Immediately the hospital fell into a more casual rhythm. It wasn't hard to guess who was the hard taskmaster around here, Cari thought. Rod didn't seem the sort of man to drive either himself or his staff to the limit.

Liz and one of the junior nurses appeared soon after Blair had left. The young nurse was carrying a sturdy walking-frame.

'Dr Kinnane wants you on your feet,' Liz said briskly. 'This is a walking-frame.'

Cari raised her eyebrows, but bit back the sarcastic comment that sprang to mind. Liz McKinley treated her as if she had the IQ of a child—a particularly stupid child at that!

It was a grim little session. With a nurse on either side of her Cari managed to find her feet. The room swam. Pain shot through her legs from her damaged pelvis. She forced herself to take a few tentative steps, and then a few more, to the door and back again, but as she reached the bed she was almost crying in pain. If it had been Maggie watching her she would have been in tears, Cari thought grimly. She was darned if she was going to cry in front of Liz McKinley, though.

White and sweating, she finally reached her bed again. A pillow had never felt so good.

'We'll try again this afternoon, shall we?' Liz said cheerfully. The walking-frame was propped against the bed where Cari could be reminded of its presence for the rest of the day, and the two nurses disappeared.

Rod put his nose around the corner of the room some time later. He eyed Cari with sympathy. 'Pain-killer?' he queried.

'Yes, please.' Cari's resolve had been broken.

The pain was just starting to ease when the hospital stirred into life again. The radio operator summoned Rod and, ten minutes later, the four-wheel-drive ambulance at the front of the hospital was being gunned into action. Rod and the ambulance staff were heading out of town.

'What's wrong?' Cari asked the aide bringing round the morning teas.

The girl put down Cari's coffee. 'There's an old man who lives about thirty kilometres out west from here,' she said. 'His wife radioed to say she thinks he's having a heart attack. She's bringing him in, but Dr Daniels is going with the ambulance to meet her. He doesn't like to leave the hospital without a doctor, but it sounds pretty bad.' She smiled at Cari. 'I've instructions from Dr Daniels to tell you all that no one's to get sick while he's away!'

Very reassuring, Cari thought wryly. This base needed three doctors. It just wasn't workable with two. What would happen when either Blair or Rod wanted time off? It was bad enough now.

There was worse to come. After she had finished her coffee, the painkiller started to work and she lay back and waited for the familiar boredom to overtake her.

The sound of a vehicle approaching at speed broke the stillness. For a moment Cari thought it must be the ambulance returning, but the times didn't fit. Rod hadn't been away long enough. There was the sound of screeching brakes and people running, then Maggie's voice raised in fear.

Cari was sure it was Maggie. The voice was unmistakable. It wasn't the sound of a professional nurse, however. It was the sound of a parent, desperately afraid.

Cari twisted on the bed, trying to see the sisters' station. It was deserted. Whatever it was had made them all run. Cari lay back and forced herself to listen. As soon as she did, above the sounds of urgency and fear in the adults was the harsh indrawing stridor of a child, desperately trying to breathe.

Cari lay perfectly still. Croup, she thought. And then, as the child on the stretcher was wheeled close to the door of her ward and she heard the faint stridor more clearly, she caught her breath. She had heard that sound before. Not croup. . . It was weakening, even as she listened.

There wasn't a doctor here. The thought tore at her and made her push the bedclothes to one side. It had to be a foreign body. That or epiglottitis.

For a moment she hesitated in indecision. How could she go in there? She was no longer a practising doctor.

A man's harsh voice and then Maggie again, sobbing in desperation. The stridor had faded to non-existence. There was no decision to make. Without her, Cari knew the child would die. She pulled herself into a sitting position, swung her legs over the side of the bed and seized the walking-frame.

Somehow she managed to get herself into a standing position. The remembered pain shot through her hips. This time, though, she was not going to give in to it. Thank heaven for the painkillers she had taken less than an hour ago, she thought briefly. The edges of the knifing pain were dulled. Slowly she shuffled forward.

The door of the ward seemed miles away, but finally she reached it and stood still, trying to gain her bearings. Two doors down, through an open door, came the sound of frightened sobbing, and Cari knew where the child had been taken. Leaving the comforting solidity of her wall, she forced herself to take those few short steps. Finally she could see.

It was a boy, eight or nine years old. Liz was working frantically with the oxygen mask. Beside her, Maggie and a big, brawny man who must be her husband watched in fear.

Cari paused at the door of the room. Only for a

moment, though. From where she stood she could see the fight was nearly over. The coughing had stopped and the child was limp and glassy-eyed.

She took a deep breath, took a firmer grip on her walking-frame and crossed to the bed. She lightly touched the child's body. It was burning hot to touch. His temperature must be forty plus.

As she touched the little boy, Liz suddenly became aware of her presence. She was holding the mask to the boy's face, with the oxygen on full.

'Get out of here,' she said harshly to Cari. She motioned savagely to the junior nurse at the doorway. 'Get her out!'

'I'm a doctor,' Cari said urgently. She held out a hand. 'Give me the mask.'

Liz stared in amazement, then with a swift gesture she shoved Cari's outstretched hand away.

'I don't know what you're playing at,' she spat, 'but you can just get back to your ward!'

'Please.' Cari took a deep breath. When she spoke again it was with all the authority she could muster. She looked up at Maggie and the big man beside her. 'It's true,' she said urgently. 'I am a doctor. I'm fully qualified and registered. I think your son's suffering from epiglottitis. Unless you let me help, he's going to choke to death.' On the trolley, the little boy's figure was pale and still.

'I don't believe you,' Liz gasped.

Maggie did, though. With her eyes not leaving her son's face she moved forward and grasped the mask from Liz's hand.

'Can you do something?' she begged.

Cari pushed her walking-frame hard against the trolley. Ignoring Liz and ignoring the savage messages the lower half of her body was giving her, she placed her fingers inside the little boy's mouth. Liz made an involuntary movement forward to prevent her. Behind her, sensing that here, in this unlikely slip of a girl, was a faint hope for his son, the big man moved and caught Liz back from the table. A hushed silence fell on the room.

There was nothing in the child's mouth. Cari hadn't expected it. The chance of the blockage being a foreign body was remote, with a temperature as high as the little boy's, but she had to check.

'Get me the anaesthetic trolley,' she ordered, hoping desperately that some procedures and basic equipment were standard worldwide. She looked up at the young nurse at the doorway. 'Move!'

The girl moved.

Twenty seconds later Cari had what she wanted—an endotracheal tube and laryngoscope. She looked down at the apparatus in her hand. She had done this before. If only her legs would support her.

They had to. They had no choice. She took a deep breath, blocked out the pain and the wide-eyed people around her, and concentrated on getting the laryngoscope into position and the slim tube down the boy's throat. There was total silence in the room. Cari eased the tube further and further in, feeling the resistance and adjusting with care. With relief, she felt it finally slide into place. It was a simple operation, if you knew how.

'Do you have humidified oxygen?' she demanded.

Liz was too dumbfounded to speak, but Maggie was with her every step of the way. A cylinder appeared, and the tube was hooked to the life-giving air.

Cari stood back. There was little she could do now. Had she been in time? Her eyes didn't waver from the limp face. Slowly, slowly the awful blue faded and a tiny amount of colour crept back into the cheeks. The child's breathing deepened and stabilised.

It was all Cari had been waiting for. As his colour came back, so hers receded. The room seemed suddenly unbearably hot. The heat rose in waves around her, mingling with the pain. The people in the room were a confused blur, their faces merging into one. Cari reached blindly to grip the walking-frame. Her hand met thin air and she crumpled into a dead faint.

When she woke she was in bed again. She opened her eyes to see concerned faces looking down. Behind a frightened little nurse was a big man—Maggie's husband, she thought vaguely.

'Is he all right?' she asked as the room came clearly back into view.

The nurse managed a glimmer of a smile. She really was very young, Cari thought.

'He's fine,' she managed.

Cari managed a weak smile. Her pelvis was on fire. She had asked her broken bones to do the impossible, and they had.

'He needs intravenous chloramphenicol,' she forced herself to say. She looked up at the nurse. 'He should be on it now. Is Dr Daniels back?'

'The ambulance is just coming in now.' Outside they could hear the sound of the vehicle pulling up at the Casualty entrance.

'Tell him,' Cari said tiredly. It was becoming a strain to speak. 'I should have put the drip up myself,' her voice faltered, 'but I couldn't.'

As the girl disappeared she looked up at the man beside the bed.

'Did you pick me up?' she managed to say. 'I'm grateful.'

The big man reached out, took her hand and gripped it fiercely. 'It's me that's grateful.' He cast a worried look at the door. He was clearly aching to be back with his son.

'He'll be fine,' Cari said, as firmly as she could. 'His breathing can't block with that tube in place.' She smiled wearily. 'Go and see.'

Fifteen minutes later a worried Rod Daniels strode into the ward. His easygoing good humour had slipped and he looked strained and tense. He strode to the bed and stood there, looking at the white face on the pillow before him. Clearly he was at a loss.

'I guess I owe you one,' he said finally.

Cari met his look. She smiled faintly. 'It was a pleasure.'

'I'll bet,' he said morosely. 'Playing doctor with a broken pelvis. . .' He broke off. 'Are you really a doctor?' he demanded.

She nodded.

Rod shook his head in disbelief. 'Well,' he exclaimed, 'what do you know! You saved his life, you realise,' he added. He grimaced. 'Kinnane's going to have my hide, and I can't say I blame him.'

'Why?' Cari was trying to block out the pain she was in. The last thing she wanted to do was listen to Rod Daniels' recriminations.

'There's always got to be someone here,' he said savagely.

'You weren't to know something like this would happen,' she said quietly. 'And you had to go.'

He shook his head. 'You know what it was?' he asked bitterly. 'Indigestion. And even if it had been a full-blown heart attack, I should have either contacted Blair to intercept him or left it to the ambulance boys.

I just took a risk.' He laughed bitterly. 'I'm too damned fond of excitement,' he acknowledged. 'If you hadn't been here. . .'

'But I was,' Cari said gently. 'Have you set up a drip?'

He nodded. 'Chloramphenicol. We should see that swelling respond within a few hours. He's going to be fine.' His voice was still morose. 'I've also given him a sedative in case he recovers enough to want to pull the tube out.'

'Rod?'

'Mmm.' He was still staring into middle distance, deep in thought.

'Do you think you could give me something too?' she pleaded.

'What? Oh. . . Are you hurting?'

'Just a bit,' Cari said faintly.

It was late afternoon when Blair returned from his clinic. From where she lay, Cari could hear his arrival. She hadn't stirred since her efforts of the morning. She was starting to believe that she had done some real damage, the pain was so severe. As she heard Blair return, her panic eased. The reassurance of his presence had no basis, but was real nevertheless.

Vaguely she could hear him at the sisters' station and then Rod's voice, and Liz and Maggie. There was little from Blair. Clearly he was content to listen.

When he finally strode into her room he was alone. The woman in the next bed had visitors and they'd put the screen up to give them privacy. Blair walked directly over to Cari and stood looking down at her. There was a long silence.

'Well?' Cari asked at last. 'Aren't you going to ask if I'm really a doctor too?'

'No.' He was watching the drawn face beneath him. 'Did Rod check you over?' he demanded.

She shook her head. 'No,' she whispered.

'Maggie said you fell—hard. Do you think you've done any damage?'

'I might have.' Her voice was a whisper.

He put a hand down and touched her face, as one would comfort a frightened child. His deep grey eyes held reassurance, comfort and concern. 'Let's find out, then, shall we?' He smiled gently down at her and Cari was suddenly lost in the tenderness of his look. She gazed up at him, her eyes widening in shock.

He too was caught. It was as if there was some invisible bond holding their eyes together, locking them in something that neither of them wanted, that neither could acknowledge or understand.

Cari's mind swelled with panic. She wrenched her gaze away and brought her hand up to cover her eyes. Let him think it was pain. . . Let him think it was anything. . .

Please, she was saying helplessly to herself. Please let the pain not be starting all over again. Please let me not be falling in love with Blair Kinnane.

The silence was endless, stretching on and on. Cari couldn't break it. It was just her, she told herself. This tension couldn't also be coming from Blair. How could he be feeling anything other than that she was a patient, and a difficult one at that?

'Right.' Blair's tone was suddenly harsh, breaking the stillness. His eyes when she met them were flint-hard, almost repelling. The professional mask was in place. 'Let's get you X-rayed.'

CHAPTER FIVE

To CARI'S intense relief the X-rays showed Blair that she had incurred no further damage. The pain she was feeling was caused by pressure on bones that weren't sufficiently healed to take it, he told her. The fractures were still stable. She was wheeled back into the ward almost light-headed with relief. An operation to reset an unstable fracture was the last thing she needed.

The big gash on her leg had opened slightly where she had knocked it on falling. It had bled, but was healed sufficiently already for it not to be a problem.

'Now,' Blair said quietly as he adjusted the dressing, 'twenty-four hours flat on your back and you'll be back to where you were yesterday.' He looked at the walking-frame beside the bed. 'I'll take that away, just in case you get any more silly ideas.'

'Silly?' Cari's voice rose in indignation.

The rigid professionalism dropped slightly and he smiled. 'Well, if you look at it from the point of view of a doctor trying to get your pelvis back together, then it was a bloody stupid idea.' Then he relented. 'From Jamie's point of view, though, there was nothing silly about it at all. Jamie Brompton's a lucky young man.'

'I'll bet he doesn't think so at the moment,' Cari said wearily.

'Jamie's not thinking anything at the moment. He's dead to the world. And his throat seems to be improving already.'

Cari nodded. The chloramphenicol could often start things improving within six hours.

46

Blair was looking at her strangely. 'Maggie says you're—how did she put it?—fully qualified and registered. Why aren't you practising?'

Cari put her head deeper into the pillow and closed her eyes firmly. 'Perhaps I'm just not interested in medicine,' she said flatly.

For a long moment he stayed looking down at her. She was intensely aware of his presence, but kept her eyes firmly closed. She didn't want questions.

'Goodnight, then, Cari,' he said finally, softly. Then he was gone. Cari listened to his footsteps echoing down the corridor. To her dismay, all she could feel was a desperate, aching want. She needed those footsteps to return, bring Blair back to her.

Footsteps sounded again, but lighter, and a junior nurse walked in.

'Dr Kinnane says you can have a sleeping tablet if you want it tonight,' she said.

'Yes, please,' Cari said wearily. Her mind was a confused jumble of pain and emotion. Perhaps sleep was the answer.

Blair had been right. The next morning Cari woke feeling slightly improved, and for the few days after that her improvement was consistent. By the end of the week she was back on the walking-frame again, and moving around the hospital almost with ease.

Subtly, the atmosphere around her had changed. It was as if, by her announcing that she was a doctor, people saw her in a different light.

She saw little of Blair. As she improved she had few needs of his professional assistance, and his visits were restricted to a formal 'look-in' each night and morning. As Cari listened to him chatting easily to other patients she experienced stabs of jealousy, furiously suppressed. It was as if he was keeping things with her strictly on a professional doctor-patient basis. Just as well, she told herself savagely. If she was being a fool it was just as well he was holding her in dislike.

The confined hospital environment was closing in on her. Cari waded through the limited hospital 'library' of paperbacks, practised her walking and stared at the ceiling.

Rod was a constant visitor, forever finding excuses to pop into her ward.

'Where did you do your training?' he demanded.

Cari told him and he whistled. 'Well! There's nothing wrong with that,' he said firmly, and she smiled.

'What did you expect?' she asked him. 'That I did medicine at a university giving doctorates in basket-weaving?'

He laughed. 'I didn't say that.'

'You implied it,' she retorted.

He shook his head. Then as Blair entered the room behind him he turned to face the older man.

'Do you know where this girl springs from?' He outlined the reputation of Cari's medical school for the benefit of the Australian. 'She could get her registration here any time she wanted it,' he said confidently.

Cari smiled. 'And why would I want to do that?' she asked, looking up at the two men.

'So you could help out here, of course,' Rod said enthusiastically. 'Couldn't she, Blair?'

Blair looked at her appraisingly, his grey eyes cool. 'Are you bored, then, Cari?'

Cari flushed. Blair Kinnane left her in no doubt as to what he thought of her. Even the knowledge that she had trained as a doctor didn't alter it. He assumed that work, for Cari, was an optional extra, something she would do when nothing better offered.

'I don't practise,' she told him.

'Why not?' Blair's question hung in the stillness of the little ward.

Cari took a deep breath.

'Because my negligence caused a death in the United States,' she said harshly. 'If you can be bothered to look up the Californian court records you'll see that negligence was proven against one Dr Cari Eliss. My lack of care killed a child. Now, if you don't mind, the subject is closed.'

Rod shook his head in stunned amazement. Blair's eyes didn't leave Cari's face.

'You told Maggie you were registered,' he said. 'Was that a lie?'

Cari shook her head miserably. 'No.'

'You weren't struck off?'

'Look, can we leave it?' Her voice broke. She took a grip on herself and glared at Blair. Once again she was aware of the undercurrent of tension running between them. Rod might as well not have been in the room. 'It's nothing to do with you,' she continued defiantly. 'I didn't intend to ever have anything to do with medicine again. If Jamie hadn't been so desperately ill, I wouldn't have.'

'Would you consider doing our radio clinics for us?'

Blair's abrupt question startled them all. Cari gasped and stared. Finally she shook her head.

'You heard what I said. I don't practise.'

Blair nodded. ' I heard.' He shrugged uninterestedly. 'If we weren't desperate, I wouldn't ask you.'

'Why desperate?' she queried.

'You've been in this place for over a fortnight now,' he said harshly. 'You know the sorts of pressures we're under. This place is funded for four doctors and we're stretching to the limit with two. What happened with

Jamie was just one of a series of problems that have occurred.'

Cari shook her head again. 'I told you,' she repeated, 'I no longer practise.'

He eyed her grimly. 'And you've told us why. Surely if we're prepared to take you on those conditions——'

'No!' It was practically a yell.

'Cari, you owe us.'

Her eyes widened in amazement, as she looked up at the cold grey eyes watching her.

'I beg your pardon?'

'If it wasn't for the Flying Doctor Service you'd be dead, and you know it. We're not asking that you devote yourself to medicine. We're asking that for the next six weeks, while you're tied to the town, you take routine radio clinics, that's all.'

'That's unfair,' Cari said quietly.

Blair nodded. 'I know.' He smiled suddenly, and once again she was caught by the change in his face. When Blair Kinnane smiled her heart felt as if it no longer belonged to her. She caught frantically for self-control, for the strength to keep her face calm and non-committal. 'I'll use threats and I'll use blackmail,' Blair continued. 'I'll use anything I can get my hands on to keep this base staffed.'

'He will too,' Rod said morosely from behind him. He mimicked Blair's voice. '"The most exciting job in the world, Dr Daniels. And the climate is unbelievable. Year-long swimming. . ." What he failed to mention was that the swimming was in the Bromptons' house dam, which you get at by crossing three hundred metres of dried mud.'

Cari smiled, but shook her head. 'I can't.'

Blair looked at her for a long moment. 'You can.' He met her gaze. Strong grey eyes caught and held, challenging her. 'You're facing six weeks of enforced idleness. As your prescribing doctor I've decided that you need something to take you mind off yourself for a change. With your permission I'll ring the Australian registration board this morning and get you registration to practise here.'

'No!' Cari wailed.

'Why not?'

'Because. . .Because. . .'

He smiled again. 'You'll have to do better than that, Dr Eliss,' he said, and left the room.

In the end Cari enjoyed it. She didn't know what strings Blair pulled to get her registration through, but three days later she was seated in front of a huge complex-looking radio, trying to follow Blair's instructions.

'It's simple,' he explained, once again overriding her objections as if they didn't exist. He and Rex, the operator, had already explained the technicalities of the vast grey beast in front of them. Cari's head was swimming.

'Every home or station using our services has a medical kit like this.' He gestured to a large box over in the corner of the room. 'It's kept fully up to date, all the time.' He handed her a list of numbered items. 'There are over a hundred items here, and you should find everything available for a normal clinic.'

Cari looked down.

'Item number 119, promethazine, mixture, 5mg. per 5 ml., 100ml. per bottle. . .2 bottles'
Item number 204, eye pad, sterile, singles. . .6——'

The list certainly looked comprehensive.

'How do patients describe symptoms, though?' she

asked uncertainly. She thought back to her time work-ing in casualty as an intern. People saying they had chest or stomach pain could mean they had pain anywhere from the neck to the groin.

Blair handed her another chart. On it were the front and rear views of the human body, mapped into areas of clinical importance and clearly labelled.

'Each station has a copy of this,' he said briskly. 'The back's easy. The patients are looking at it from the same view as it actually is. For the front you have to ensure that they're not giving you the mirror image of where their pain is. If there's any doubt, get them to put the chart on their chest and look down. That way they can't make a mistake.'

'Surely they can't confuse left and right?' Cari asked, startled.

Blair smiled. 'These people are often elderly, iso-lated, ill and confused,' he reminded her. 'It's up to you to get it clear, not them.'

She nodded. 'And what if they sound as if they should be seen?'

Blair gestured to Rex, standing behind them. 'Rex is an old hand at this. You tell him what you want done, and if you think it warrants immediate ambulance service he'll organise it. If you think it should be seen within the next week, then he knows the dates and places of all the clinics and whether a special one has to be arranged. He also knows the situations of most of these people—whether they have means of getting themselves here or not, whether they have people around them who can be depended on to give them adequate care. Anything you need, just ask Rex.'

Cari looked around and smiled at the elderly man behind her. It sounded as if she would be depending on him.

'I'll make sure I'm available for the first couple of sessions,' Blair further reassured her. 'If you need me, Rex will come and get me.' He looked at his watch. 'I've got a patient coming in now—I have to admit.'

'Nothing else I need to know?' asked Cari.

'I don't think so. The first calls should start coming through any minute now.'

'OK,' she said nervously.

He smiled reassuringly. 'Just don't talk for too long,' he reminded her. 'Some of these people are very isolated and very lonely. If they can, they'll talk for half an hour, and there may be urgent calls waiting. You have to be a bit ruthless, I'm afraid. They've got the galah session for chat.'

'Galah session?' she echoed.

'Named after one of our noisiest native birds,' he smiled. 'We open the radio network to allow "neighbours" to chat—even though they may be hundreds of kilometres apart.'

He glanced at his watch again, and once again Cari caught an unmistakable message. Blair Kinnane wished to spend not one moment more with her than he absolutely must.

'I have to go,' he said decisively. He looked down at her, his face growing serious. 'Welcome back to the medical profession, Dr Eliss. You're on your own.'

As he walked out of the door Cari stared in panic. Then she caught herself and turned back to the big grey beast in front of her.

Rex opened the session with a short introductory message to any of the stations tuned in. It felt odd, Cari thought, to sit in this equipment-packed radio-room and imagine all the different people in remote areas learning for the first time of a new woman doctor at Slatey Creek.

The calls, when they came in, were laced with curiosity and often hesitant.

As Blair had reassured her, it was routine stuff. Children with high temperatures or sore ears, old ladies with arthritic pain, people caring for chronically ill relatives, sprains and bruises associated with farm work. . . Occasionally there was something more serious. Cari found them clearly recognisable.

There was an elderly man whose abscess on his leg sounded as if it needed attention. Cari queried Rex. There was no one with him who could take adequate care of him—in fact, he was attempting to take care of a wife who was more frail than he.

'We'll arrange for the plane to pick them both up this afternoon,' Rex told her.

The last call for the morning was for ante-natal advice. As Cari signed off she glanced at her watch. With a shock she realised she'd been on the radio for two hours. She shifted on her stool and a sharp twinge of pain shot through her pelvis. She'd forgotten it for the entire time she was working.

Working. . . She settled back into her hospital bed with a satisfied feeling of having done something useful. For the first time in twelve months she'd done the job she'd been trained to.

Was this going to make it worse? She closed her eyes wearily, tired by her morning's efforts. She had vowed never to practise medicine again. All this job was going to do was remind her how much she was missing being a doctor. In six weeks, when she moved on, there would still be nothing.

She was half expecting, half hoping that Blair would drop in to talk about her morning's work. Once again, though, he didn't come near her. It was as if she had the plague, she thought bitterly, then corrected herself.

If she'd had the plague she knew Blair Kinnane would turn again into a concerned and sympathetic doctor.

She fell asleep depressed and slept until Maggie woke her halfway through the afternoon. Her body was still reacting to its battering by demanding almost eighteen hours of sleep a day.

'Wake up, sleepyhead,' Maggie said cheerfully. She was obviously here for a visit rather than work. Her big bright skirt and blouse proclaimed that she was on holiday. 'If I thought you were expecting a dozen visitors tonight I'd let you sleep, but I suspect I'm the only visitor you're going to get.'

Cari opened her eyes and smiled. It was good to see Maggie's cheerful face again. She pushed herself upright and welcomed her visitor with delight. Maggie reached into a capacious bag and produced a tiny box of strawberries.

'Mmm!' Cari picked one of the luscious red fruits up and popped it into her mouth. In this harsh climate such delicacies were almost unheard-of. 'How on earth did you get these?'

'I grow them myself,' Maggie said proudly. 'In a pot in the back veranda. Actually,' she confided, her pride increasing, 'I told Jamie he could have the ripe ones this week and he decided that you should have them. Or most of them,' she corrected herself scrupulously.

'How is he?' asked Cari.

'Full of self-importance since we brought him home,' Maggie admitted. 'He's the only kid he knows who's nearly died. David's madly jealous.'

'The infection's subsided?'

Maggie nodded.

'Are you coming back to work, then?'

'No, not for a while.' Maggie settled back into the chair beside Cari's bed. 'I'm due for holidays anyway, so I thought I'd take a few weeks and just give Jamie a bit of extra attention.' She grinned. 'Besides, the place is a hell-hole, and if I don't do some spring-cleaning soon the dust will claim victory. So I'm home, awaiting visitors. When are you coming?'

'I'm not sure,' Cari said slowly. 'Do you still want me?'

'Of course we do,' Maggie said firmly. 'We all do.' She reached over and took Cari's hands between hers. 'You've given us a very special gift,' she said softly. 'We want you to come.'

Cari smiled. 'I'm not sure if I can, though,' she said slowly. She told Maggie what she had agreed to do.

'No problem,' Maggie said expansively. 'Stay here until you're fit to drive a car for a few minutes each day and then come on out. When I'm not working, my little sedan isn't used. You can settle in at home and just come in here when you're needed.'

'It sounds ideal.'

'It is ideal. That's settled, then. Now. . .' Maggie foraged deeper into her bag and produced a toilet bag and a couple of nighties. Cari recognised them with delight.

'My things!' she exclaimed. 'How did you get them?'

'Your truck has finally arrived in town and is sitting down at the garage waiting for the insurance assessor to visit. Jock saw it there when he was in town yesterday, pulled out the suitcase and brought it home. We've got it all. The only problem is that it was open and is chock full of red dust. These were all I could get cleaned in time to bring in today.'

'That's fine,' said Cari. 'If you knew how much I hate these hospital nightgowns. . . I don't need the rest.'

'So what about Saturday night?'

'Saturday night?'

'The Slatey Creek hospital dinner dance,' Maggie explained.

'You've got to be kidding,' Cari protested. 'You're not suggesting that I go?'

'You've got six days' recuperation before then,' Maggie said. 'The whole district comes in for it, and everyone's dying to meet you. It's a great method of letting them inspect you. Otherwise I'll have them dropping in on us on the flimsiest excuse for weeks. Especially the men,' she added reflectively.

'But it's crazy! I can't dance. I have trouble sitting for more than a couple of hours.'

'And that's all you'll have to do,' Maggie said firmly. 'I've already checked with Blair and he can't see any reason why not. Jock and I will pick you up and will bring you back here as soon as you say the word.' She stood up. 'I don't want to be personal. . .'

'It sounds like you're going to be anyway.'

'Don't interrupt.' Maggie frowned severely. 'You're becoming introverted and miserable, and I've decided it's my mission in life to spread a little joy in your existence.' She glowered at Cari. 'And I don't take lightly my missions being interfered with. You hear?'

'Yes, ma'am.'

'Then you'll come?'

'Have I a choice?' sighed Cari.

'No.'

Cari grinned and spread her hands helplessly. 'Then your kind invitation is accepted with pleasure.'

Maggie laughed. 'Great.' She closed her bag and stood up. 'You won't regret it. And if you're wondering what you can wear, I discovered a lovely white dress in the bottom of your case. At least,' she said reflectively, 'it was once white. I'm working on it. If I don't get it right by Saturday I'll just dye it red.'

'The white dress?' Cari was startled. 'Isn't that too formal?'

'We're a very formal lot at Slatey Creek,' Maggie retorted.

CHAPTER SIX

BY THE time Saturday night arrived Cari had deserted the walking-frame in favour of a heavy walking stick. She still felt about a hundred with it in her hand, but there was no escaping its necessity.

Maggie had brought in her dress the night before, and Cari surveyed the remembered garment with mixed feelings. It was a soft, sheer silk, flowing over an almost non-existent under-dress. It was the dress she had worn the night she became engaged to Harvey. She had thrown it into her suitcase at the last minute just in case. . . Just in case what? The answer to her self-questioning eluded her.

She had lost weight in the last few weeks. The dress had looked lovely on her before; with the new, slim Cari the effect was almost ethereal. Her eyes were too big for her face, she thought dispassionately, large pools of colour on her too pale complexion. She brushed her hair until it shone, and let it hang free. Harvey had thought it immature to wear it like that. With him she had braided it, or caught it back in a soft roll. She caught it up and stared at her reflection before letting it loose again. The Cari who had been engaged to Harvey Wells no longer existed.

Maggie and Jock arrived to collect her. It was strange leaving the hospital, and suddenly Cari felt immensely nervous. These walls had been her home for the past three weeks or so. It seemed a huge step, suddenly, to leave their safe confines.

It was dark when they left the hospital building, but

she could make out a little of the town. It consisted of one long dusty street, with buildings set well back. There were a few straggly trees that looked as if they were struggling to survive. There appeared to be little else.

The dinner was being held in the local hall. It was only a few hundred metres from the hospital, but, in deference to Cari's broken bones, Jock drove the girls to the door. The mill of people around the door separated to let them through. Cari walked self-consciously at Maggie's side, suddenly aware that she was the focus of attention.

As Maggie had said, it was a good way to get this over with. If she had to be inspected by the population, at least she could be inspected by everyone at the same time!

It wasn't such an ordeal as she had anticipated. People were only too eager to assist her. Jock and Maggie had arranged to sit at a table reserved for the hospital staff and their partners, and before long she was seated and surrounded by faces, many of which she found familiar. After more than three weeks in the hospital, most of the staff felt like old friends. Rod was there, and Rex, and Blair with Liz.

Blair and Liz were seated at the far end of the table. Cari was conscious of Blair's swift, appraising glance as she walked to the table. Then he turned back, to laugh at something his lovely partner had just said.

Rod was nearer to where she was seated.

'How can you all be off duty?' Cari demanded.

'Have a heart!' groaned Rod. 'We're only three hundred metres from the place, after all.' He motioned to a mobile radio receiver lying on the end of the table. 'We're within two minutes of the hospital. Sometimes that has to be enough.'

Cari smiled and relaxed. The food was plain but good, and the company cheerful. As the meal concluded the band started up. Cari's feet were itching, but she was forced to sit and watch as the couples whirled around the dance-floor.

There was no shortage of company. This was a district where the men far outnumbered the women. Even though Cari's walking stick told prospective partners that she was off limits as far as dancing went, she was never left alone. One young man after another vied for her attention.

The women too were eager to talk, and Cari realised just how starved of new faces this group of people were. She realised ruefully that her dress was being examined from all angles and she knew she would be a topic of conversation over the 'galah session' for some time to come. Many of these people had been driving all day to get here—some had even used their light planes—and any glimmer of gossip or news was soaked up avidly.

Rod deserted her as soon as the meal finished. Although it was clear that Cari intrigued him, the thought of a partner who couldn't dance was obviously not to Dr Daniels's taste. He whirled around the floor with one attractive young lady after another.

Blair danced mostly with Liz. She was dressed to kill in a clinging red satin dress which revealed her exquisite figure to perfection. Blair's dark suit was a perfect foil for her scarlet. She clung possessively to him as he moved her skilfully around the floor.

They made a handsome couple, Cari thought, trying to block the insidious jealousy stirring within her. Obviously those around her agreed with her assessment. 'We'll have wedding bells in Slatey Creek yet,' one of the young matrons said conspiratorially to Maggie.

Maggie shook her head. 'I doubt it,' she said as the woman moved away.

'Why?' Cari asked curiously.

Maggie shrugged. 'I don't think our Dr Kinnane is in the market for a wife,' she said, 'no matter how much Sister McKinley likes to throw herself at him.'

'Why not?' Cari knew she shouldn't ask, but the impulse to do so was too strong to resist.

'He's been married,' Maggie told her. 'I did my training in Melbourne at the hospital where Blair was doing his junior residency. He was married to one of the hospital social workers, and even at that time there were rumours sweeping the hospital.'

'Rumours?'

Maggie smiled grimly. 'We all knew about the Kinnanes,' she said. 'Everyone knew what Inez was doing, and everyone spent time speculating how much Blair knew of what his lovely wife was up to.'

'Whatever do you mean?' Cari had no business enquiring, but she couldn't help herself.

Maggie shrugged. 'It was all a bit sordid. I don't know why Inez married Blair, really. Certainly being married to a very junior doctor didn't suit her style. Rumour has it that his family has money. He must have been married very young, and I could see why he married her—she was an absolute stunner. Anyway, her job as a social worker seemed to be just an excuse to come into contact with every good-looking or power-ful man in the hospital.' Maggie grimaced. 'Certainly in the time I was there she had at least three affairs.'

'So they divorced?'

'The divorce happened after I'd left to marry Jock,' Maggie said. 'I guess finally he saw what everyone else in the hospital had been seeing. All I know is that now, ten years later, the last thing Blair Kinnane seems to be looking for is another wife.' She looked across to where Blair was smiling down at Liz. 'He amuses himself, certainly, but he always seems to pick the tough ones, the ones that angle after him and aren't likely to be hurt.' She hesitated. 'I guess a betrayal like that would take a lifetime to get over.'

Cari nodded thoughtfully. So Blair Kinnane had been hurt too. She looked across at him and, to her dismay, was caught. Blair looked up at the wrong moment and met her eye. Once again the tension surfaced, palpable across the crowded dance-floor. Cari turned a deep crimson and averted her gaze.

All of a sudden she was tired. The band struck up a slow waltz and the couples on the floor moved closer to each other. Jock appeared, to claim his wife.

'Do you think you could run me back to the hospital after this dance?' Cari asked him.

'Sure. We can go now if you like.'

As Jock spoke Blair appeared from the dance-floor. Looking up, Cari realised that Liz had been claimed by another partner.

'Going already?' He smiled at Cari and her heart gave a sickening lurch. What was she doing? After Harvey she had sworn never to become involved with another man, and yet here she was, flushing like a teenager with her first crush.

'I'm tired,' she said quietly.

He was close now, forced by the crowd of people to stand hard against her looking down.

'But this is my dance.'

Cari shook her head. 'You know I'm not dancing,' she said curtly. She took her stick from the back of the chair and stood up.

Blair smiled over at Jock. 'That's a challenge if ever I heard one,' he laughed. 'Go and dance with your wife, Jock. I'll look after Cari.'

Before Cari knew what he was about, the stick had been removed from her hand. Blair's arms were around her and she was half lifted out on to the dance-floor.

She made an involuntary protest, pushing him away. For answer, she was just held tighter.

'If I were you I wouldn't struggle,' he smiled down at her. 'If I let you go you'll fall over.'

She would too. Baffled, she subsided.

'That's better.' He adjusted his hold, and let the music dictate his movements. 'Relax,' he said softly. 'I'm taking your weight. Just let me do the work.'

Cari looked up wonderingly into the tanned face above her, and then down. There was no help for it. She buried her face in Blair's broad shoulder and let him dance with her.

They danced in the age-old way of lovers. His hands were around her, under her arms, clasping her body hard against him. When he moved, Cari was forced to follow. For a couple of moments she felt clumsy, unsure, but as the music took hold and Blair's strength gave her confidence she relaxed. Momentarily she thought of Liz. Surely the girl would object to Blair holding another woman in this way? Then the nearness of Blair's body, the smell and feel of him, drove out every other thought.

Around they went, around the crowded dance hall, with Cari's feet hardly touching the ground. Blair was strong and skilled. His body was hard and lean against ̱ut moulding in to fit her slight body against his ̱ ̱pporting her totally. Dexterously he ̱ ̱er without touching the other dancers. ̱ f she was dancing better than she had ever danced, a weightless, involuntary movement, the perfect merging of two bodies.

She was lost, swirling in a hazy mist of desire. These strong arms around her, the faint masculine aroma of Blair Kinnane, this body was all that mattered. The music softened and receded. Around them other dancers passed in a blur. Cari was conscious only of Blair.

As the music faded and stopped, she looked up into the face of the man above her. Her face reflected her confusion. Her eyes met Blair's deep grey ones, and they read the same uncertainty. For a long moment they stayed locked together, each unwilling to break the moment.

With a blast, the band started the next number. Obviously they had done their romantic piece for the evening and now wanted the dancers moving again. It was heavy rock.

Blair didn't move. Around them the dancers broke into the rhythm of rock. Still he was watching Cari, his face still and questioning.

'Take me back, please.' Cari said the words uncertainly. His hands still held her and without his support she could go nowhere.

'Is that what you want?' His smile made her heart rise and swell so that she could hardly speak.

She forced herself to smile back. 'If you try me with this number we'll both end up on the floor! For rock you need four skilled legs, not two.'

He nodded reluctantly. 'Well, you owe me a dance, Dr Eliss. I'll hold you to it.'

'You'll be waiting a while,' Cari warned.

He looked at her appraisingly, then nodded. 'I can wait,' he said.

*   *   *

An hour later Cari was back between sheets in her hospital ward. Behind the door the white dress hung, its purpose over. It looked wrong, out of place in this place of sickness, she thought.

On Monday Jock was going to bring in the little sedan and, if she found she could drive it, she would go back out to the station. Meanwhile, there were two more nights of hospital for her to get through.

The dance was still going strong. From where she lay she could hear the band, playing for all they were worth. What they lacked in quality they made up for in volume, she thought wryly.

Sleep wouldn't come. Her legs ached from their unaccustomed use. She told herself firmly that the pain in her legs was the only reason for not sleeping. She knew, though, that there was another, stronger reason.

She felt betrayed by her own body, her own mind. Blair Kinnane had left her in no doubt as to his opinion of her. He thought she was a spoiled rich child. Despite that, he had been kind, making her feel attractive and desirable. He was probably doing the same thing right now with Liz McKinley. Kindness was no reason to fall head over heels in love with the man. And besides, the last thing Blair Kinnane wanted was her love.

'It's only because you've been lonely and miserable,' she told herself savagely. 'Patients always fall in love with their doctors. They told us that in medical school—it's one of the hazards of the profession.'

And yet a tiny voice within her told her that it was more than that, that what she was feeling for Blair Kinnane was deeper than she had ever felt before, even for the man to whom she had once been engaged.

She pushed her head hard into the pillow and swore violently. The night sister popped her head around the door.

'Are you all right, Dr Eliss? Can I get you anything?'

Cari turned over and sighed. She shook her head. 'No, thanks Sister. I'm fine. I've got to get used to sleeping without drugs again.'

The girl nodded. 'It's up to you,' she smiled. 'Only don't make a martyr of yourself, will you?'

She went on her way, and Cari was left to stare at the darkened walls and try to will sleep to come.

Five minutes later the sound of voices in the hospital car park outside her bedroom window brought her wide awake. She knew without looking who it was. Blair and Liz. Blair lived in an apartment at the rear of the hospital. Liz lived out of town, and tonight she had brought in her car and left it, for safety, in the hospital car park.

Without even questioning the morality of what she was doing, Cari slipped out of bed and moved the curtain fractionally so she could make out the two figures standing beside the car. While she watched, Liz's arms came up around Blair's neck. For a long moment he looked down, then he bent and kissed the upturned lips.

Cari threw the curtain back into place and climbed back into bed, sick at heart and disgusted at what she had done. She pulled the bedclothes up over her face and swore, under her breath, solidly, the same word over and over again. On the three hundred and forty-seventh swear word, Dr Cari Eliss finally fell asleep.

CHAPTER SEVEN

ON MONDAY afternoon, Cari was finally able to pack her accumulated possessions and leave the hospital. She drove the short distance out of the town to Jock's and Maggie's home with her heart light with relief.

She might have felt different if this had been the end of her stay in Slatey Creek, she acknowledged to herself. In her weeks as a patient she had made some good friends. When she finally had to leave she would miss them.

When she finally had to leave. . . She questioned the form her thoughts had taken curiously. It was as if this place was growing to be part of her, this barren, remote settlement where no one came unless they had to.

It was because this place was providing her with a refuge, she told herself. It was a place where the pressures of home could not catch up with her. Despite the pain of the past few weeks, her injury had provided a welcome respite from her running. Here she had been able to stop and catch her breath after the nightmare of the past twelve months. It was as if the accident was the peak of her dreadful times. From here on in. . .

From here on in she didn't know. With Jock sitting beside her she eased the little car over the worst of the bumps, wincing at the unavoidable jolting. She knew it would be at least a month before she could travel long distances. A month with her tiny, undemanding job of running radio clinics and staying with Maggie and Jock—these people who had become her friends.

Somehow, in that month, she also had to get Blair Kinnane out of her system. She had to leave here with a whole heart. She couldn't face the future with emotional entanglements.

With surprise she thought suddenly back to Harvey. The pain of his desertion was fading to almost nothing. She shook her head in amazement. Blair Kinnane had at least given her that.

The road ahead forked. Cari looked a question at Jock and he pointed right. Jock had insisted on her driving.

'If you're going to be driving yourself in and out from town the more practice you have the better,' he'd told her.

'You don't know how much I appreciate you and Maggie doing this for me,' Cari said softly now.

He smiled, a big, open grin that lit up his face. 'You would have been welcome before,' he said roughly. 'Now you've given us our boy back, don't let's have any more talk of thanks. It's us who are doing the thanking, and we're really happy to be doing it.' He gestured to a rough track leading from the road. 'Here's home,' he said simply.

Home was a cluster of buildings set back in the dusty paddocks. The house itself was dwarfed by the number of water tanks, high on stilts around the house. It was an old weatherboard house, slightly run down, with huge verandas running all around.

Maggie was standing on the veranda, her hand to her eyes to shade the harsh glare of the sun as she watched the approaching car. As the little car pulled up she started down the wide steps, only to be edged aside by two excited small boys and what seemed a veritable pack of excited dogs. For a while there was general commotion as Maggie tried to greet Cari, the boys tried to tell her everything she should know at once, and each dog added its peculiar brand of welcome. By the time Cari's belongings were inside and the door shut firmly on children and dogs, she was breathless with laughter.

'I did warn you,' Maggie reminded her.

The Bromptons' household was like a breath of fresh air after the quiet and antiseptic cleanliness of the hospital. Before dinner that night Cari had been escorted around everything the two boys considered of importance. She had checked out the sheds and the trucks. The workings of the water pumps had been shown to her. She had even inspected the inside of the dog kennels. The children obviously went without visitors for months on end and her presence was a delight.

Their only disappointment was that Cari couldn't yet ride a horse.

'And I don't think I'm going to be able to for months,' she confessed. The thought of doing such a thing made her cringe.

'Never mind,' Jamie said grandly. 'When you get a little bit better I'll take you around the paddocks in the jeep.'

'You will?' Cari asked, startled.

Maggie smiled. 'The children learn how to handle a vehicle very young here,' she explained. 'If Jock's mending a fence he may be four kilometres from the house. If the kids want to spend some time with him, they've got to be mobile.'

'But surely they can't go on the road?'

'That's not much of a restriction around here,' Maggie told her. 'You can go for kilometres in many directions without even seeing a track.'

Cari shook her head. The vastness of this country took her breath away.

It was easy to settle in with these friendly people. She nestled into her big bed that night with pleasure. Her room was spacious, with huge windows open to let the night air circulate. They had screens to prevent insects entering, but no curtains. There was no need for privacy in this place, Cari thought. Anyone approaching the house would set the dogs barking before they could get near enough to even think of seeing through a window.

The silence as the night took over was almost eerie. Above her head the ceiling fan whirred noiselessly. Outside, a dog stirred on its chain and then was still. Cari moved contentedly in her bed and slept.

She soon adjusted to her new routine. The Bromptons were astir early. Cari soon learned that sleep was considered something people did in the dark. The household woke at dawn.

'It's the coolest part of the day,' Maggie explained. 'If I don't get things done before nine o'clock, I don't get them done at all.'

By nine the housework had been done, the animals attended to and the boys were seated by the radio, tuned in to the School of the Air. By nine, Cari tried to be on the road into Slatey Creek. It took her less than half an hour to go into the tiny settlement, but it gave her time once at the hospital to catch up with any information she needed to know before the medical clinic.

It was amazing how quickly she was learning about her outback patients. As each call came through, Rex would give her a quick summary of the patient's circumstances. Cari enjoyed imagining her patients seated behind their radio sets in their remote stations.

Many of her patients were 'regulars', sufferers from chronic illnesses such as pernicious anaemia or diabetes who were required to report in regularly. Others who were elderly and alone were also required to check in, just to let the base know that they were fit and well.

'Surely there aren't many people living alone in these remote areas?' Cari questioned Blair as she passed over her sheets of information from the morning session.

'More than I like to think of,' he said grimly. 'The young ones can't wait to get to the city. If the stations aren't paying their way, then there's no money to pay for help. What keeps some of these old-timers on the land is just sheer bloody-mindedness. And fear of the big smoke too,' he added reflectively. 'For a lot of them, Slatey Creek would hold enough people to worry them.'

Cari's conversations with Blair were rare. By the time she arrived in the mornings he was caught up with morning surgery and by the time she finished he was nearly always caught up with the demands of the frantic practice. When she had queries she learned to ask Rod. Sometimes she found herself imagining that Blair was avoiding her completely.

The first alteration to her routine came near the end of her second week out of hospital. Rod was out at one of the remote settlements. Midway during Cari's morning clinic she heard a commotion in the corridor behind her. She queried Rex with her eyes before turning her attention back to the radio and the state of Mrs Bickerton's varicose veins. Rex went to the door, took one look and disappeared from view.

Two minutes later he was back.

'Doc Kinnane says can you come,' he said urgently as Cari signed off from Mrs Bickerton. He moved to the set. 'I'll take over here.'

'But there'll still be people. . .'

'They'll have to wait,' Rex said firmly. He jerked his head towards the door. 'You're needed. Now.'

Cari frowned and stood up. She left her stick beside the machine. Unless she was walking any distance or over rough ground she could get along without it now. As she emerged into the corridor, one of the junior nurses signalled her urgently and motioned her towards Casualty.

Blair didn't look up as she entered. On the couch was a small, wiry-looking man, in his forties. He was unconscious, and one look was enough to tell Cari that he was desperately ill. Behind them was a middle-aged woman, sobbing in fear. A nurse's aide had her arms around the weeping woman and was leading her out as Cari appeared.

Blair was working frantically. With a sinking heart, Cari recognised the contents of the bottle above the level of the bed. Plasma expander. With no obvious external injury. . .

'Ruptured aortic aneurism.' Blair must have sensed her presence, but his whole attention was riveted on his patient. Without looking up, he confirmed her tentative guesswork. 'Can you gas?' he demanded.

'Gas?' Cari's query was more an attempt to get her breath than ask a question.

'Gas,' Blair said harshly. 'Give an anaesthetic. I'm going in. At least, if you've got the skills to support me, I'm going in.'

Cari shook her head in dismay. A ruptured aortic aneurism. . . A tear in the body's main blood vessel. . . Even in the big metropolitan teaching hospital the success rate for these operations was less than fifty per cent.

'Have you been in this situation before?' Blair demanded. His voice was rough, demanding an immediate response.

Cari shook her head. 'I've never been involved.'

'But you've seen it done.'

She nodded, almost reluctantly. She had spent two years training in anaesthetics. Two years of struggle for a qualification she no longer wanted. And this operation. . .

'Yes.'

She had seen attempts to repair a ruptured aortic aneurism twice before. Both times, in the major teaching hospital where she had trained, the patient had died. Sometimes, just sometimes, if the rupture wasn't too severe, if the surgeon was skilled and if they got it in time, then the patient could survive. It seemed unbelievable that, in this remote outback hospital, this little man could have any chance at all.

'Do we know his blood-group? Can we cross-match blood here?' she asked tentatively. Then, her voice becoming surer as she realised the enormity of Blair's proposal, she voiced even stronger objections. 'For heaven's sake, how much blood do you keep here? You're looking at ten units at the very least!'

One of those units was being set up as a drip as she spoke.

Blair finally looked up at her, his face set in uncompromising lines.

'Scrub, Dr Eliss,' he said harshly. 'Fast.'

'But I don't——'

'You don't what?' he demanded. He signalled to the orderly beside him. With Blair not leaving the little man's side, the trolley started to be pushed towards

Theatre. 'Joe's one of our regular donors, thank God. Not only do we have his blood-group but we have a unit of his own blood we can use. We've got three other units available, and we're going to have to risk not cross-matching. I've got someone on the phone getting every other potential donor to the hospital now.' He paused at the door to Theatre, as the trolley was manoeuvred around the doorway. 'This is no time for self-questioning, Dr Eliss. Move!'

'But. . .'

'But what? Stand back, do nothing and let him die? Is that what you're suggesting?'

Cari moved.

As she approached the table there were other questions whirling in her brain. 'Theatre staff?' she asked tentatively. She had never seen this operation attempted without at least two surgeons.

'Maggie's coming in,' Blair answered curtly. He was checking the equipment being assembled around the table. 'She's done years of theatre work in Melbourne and Perth. There's no one I'd rather have.' He glanced impatiently up at the clock on the wall. 'She should be here now.'

'But you need another doctor.' Cari's voice was almost a whisper.

'Well, I haven't got one.'

The door opened and Maggie came in. By her breathing Cari knew she had been running. They were now as ready as they were ever going to be.

Cari administered the anaesthetic almost automatically, her mind clicking smoothly back into routines that had been drilled into her until they were almost automatic. Three of the precious units of blood had already disappeared into the man's veins. Cari had no idea what was happening outside the theatre walls,

whether at the end of the next unit more would be
forthcoming. One step at a time, she told herself firmly.
She administered the lightest of anaesthetics, conscious
of the tenuous grip on life held by the man in her care.
At her signal, Blair took a deep breath, and made a
swift incision.

For a moment Cari's attention was diverted from the
dials of the anaesthetic trolley. She took a swift look
and then wished she hadn't. Surely the task Blair had
set for himself was impossible.

She couldn't watch. The patient's condition was
fragile. It was going to take all her remembered skills
to play her part. Whatever Blair did, she had to be
sure that her part was played to the full, giving the
little man every possible chance.

She looked down at the face beneath her hands. He
was too young for such a catastrophic thing as this to
happen to him, she thought dully. Then she pushed the
thought away, remembering a professor's advice years
before. 'There is no place for emotion in the operating
theatre. You let emotion in and your clear head
disappears. If you start thinking about the person, you
lose the patient.'

Blair swore softly, and Cari's glance flicked up at
him and then back to the face of her patient. Blair was
sweating. Perspiration stood out in beads from his skin.
Cari knew he would be searching desperately, trying to
reach the source of the oozing blood.

Maggie was working steadily beside him. Whatever
domestic chaos she had left behind her, as she walked
into the room she transformed into someone Cari
almost didn't recognise. There was no questioning of
her nursing skills. Blair was giving her steady orders.
His hands were fully occupied.

For this procedure to be carried out with one surgeon

was unthinkable. Blair was using Maggie as his other pair of hands. On his instructions she was putting pressure on bleeding points, pulling on retractors, ligating or clamping small blood vessels. . . On the other side of the table another sister worked just as efficiently. Blair demanded and got the best out of his staff, Cari thought fleetingly.

It wasn't going to be any use if there was no more blood. Desperately Cari's glance kept flicking up at the door, willing a nurse to come through carrying more of the precious bags. Nothing. She looked down at the huge incision. Beneath Blair's hands the blood surged and welled from the ruptured aorta. Maggie was holding the rubber suction hose, taking it away from Blair's probing fingers.

A junior nurse opened the door of the theatre. She opened her mouth to speak, but was forestalled by Cari.

'Take this and siphon it into a bag,' Cari ordered the startled girl, motioning to the container Maggie was filling.

Blair looked up, startled. For a moment his concentration was broken. 'You mean re-use it?' he asked.

'Why not?' Cari said grimly. 'It saves cross-matching.'

She had never tried to do it before, but the sight of so much blood had made her realise that it might be possible to feed back some of the oozing blood into the patient's veins. Within two minutes she had another unit hooked up, feeding into Joe's arm.

'There should be more coming within about five minutes,' the nurse told Cari, looking doubtfully down at the table. 'That's what I came in to tell you. We've got donors coming in from all over, but it takes them time to get here.'

Cari nodded. At the rate Joe was losing it she would have her bag refilled in less than no time. If only Blair could locate the tear. If it was too high. . .

She looked down at her dials and hope died within her. He was going.

'Blair,' she warned sharply.

'Damn,' he said under his breath. Then suddenly, 'Got it!' It was a cry of momentary triumph.

Another sister pushed open the swing doors of the theatre. Another unit of blood. Cari grabbed it gratefully and sent it pouring into the man's veins. She checked the dials again. The blood-pressure was responding, ever so slightly.

'I think we might. . .'

An hour later they closed. They had done their best and Joe was still alive. It was all they could say. Ahead of him lay massive problems, but there was now a chance. The gaping tear had been repaired.

Maggie went with the trolley up to the small ward which served as Slatey Creek's intensive care unit. Blair and Cari discarded their theatre garb and washed silently, both of them stunned by the events of the past few hours. It was too soon to be jubilant, Cari thought. All the same, she felt a surge of real satisfaction go through her. If Blair hadn't operated then the farmer would be dead, right at this minute. Perhaps they had only given him hours. Or perhaps they had given him twenty years.

Behind them the nurses were also subdued, as if they too recognised the enormity of the operation they had just witnessed.

This man was skilled, Cari thought. Blair Kinnane had skills which the surgeons in her training hospital

would have envied. To operate with a positive result
here. . . She turned to him impulsively.

'Congratulations, Blair.'

He dredged up a smile. The ordeal had drained him,
she thought dispassionately. He looked as though he
could use a stiff drink. She felt an almost overwhelming
urge to place her hands around his dark head and hold
his face against her, smoothing away the lines of strain
and fatigue.

Behind them the nurses were starting to clean up.
Blair finished drying his hands slowly and methodically.
'He's not out of the wood yet,' he reminded her.

'No. But you've given him a chance.'

'Correction,' he smiled down at her, the smile light-
ing the weariness of his face, 'we've given him a chance.
That was some skill you showed in there, Dr Eliss.
Rod was right when he said you'd been well trained.'

Cari flushed and shrugged.

'You've done anaesthetics.'

'Once I was going to make it a career,' she said
dully.

Blair nodded. 'I thought as much. You don't show
the skills you displayed in there after the anaesthetics
you learn in medical school.'

'Well, how about you?' Cari interrupted. 'I didn't
realise you were a surgeon.'

He nodded. 'It'd be impossible to practise out here
if I wasn't,' he said.

'You don't call yourself Mister.'

He shook his head and smiled wearily. 'The locals
don't like it. I'm Doc Kinnane to them, and no amount
of qualifications I have is going to make any difference.'
He looked at her for a moment.

'That was a clever idea you had,' he said. His eyes
were on her, warmly appraising. 'I've never seen

recycled blood before.' He grinned suddenly, triumphantly. 'I reckon the way you were pumping it into
him some of it may have gone around four times!'

Cari shook her head. She was feeling limp and shaky.
She glanced at the clock on the wall behind them. It
was over three hours since they had entered Theatre.

For a moment there was silence. Blair's momentary
triumph faded. He picked up a towel and started slowly
drying his hands.

'Why aren't you practising?' he demanded.

'I told you.'

He shook his head. 'You didn't tell me what happened.' He hesitated. 'I think it's time you did.'

Cari shook her head numbly. The old remembered
pain came flooding back. Perhaps when she explained,
then Blair Kinnane would believe her version of events.
If he did then he could well offer her a job.

Did she want it? To work again was to leave herself
open to the same catastrophic events that had turned
her world upside down in the past.

More probable than his belief, though, would be a
reaction of the same disbelief she had met before. The
same reaction of aversion and disdain. She couldn't
bear it. To risk that reaction for the sake of the chance
of a job she didn't want. . .

No, it must stay as it was. As it stood she would
work in an emergency to repay in part the debt that
she owed these people. Then it would be finished.

'No,' she said firmly.

Blair looked at her silently for a long moment. Then
he put aside his towel and turned away.

'I need to talk to Joe's wife,' he said.

Cari stayed in the hospital for another couple of hours.
Her skills were still needed. The place was busier than

she had ever seen it before. Finally, after one last check on their recovering patient, she recognised Rod's car in the car park. The sight filled her with relief. With Rod's return it was safe for her to go home.

She turned to walk down the hospital corridor. Outside Blair's office she paused. The voices of Rod and Blair were carrying clearly, and equally clear was their topic of conversation. They were talking about her.

'So why don't we offer her a job?' Rod's voice was unmistakable.

'How can we?' Blair's voice was echoing the strain from the morning.

'How can we not?' Rod was exasperated. 'Look at you, man! You're exhausted. You were up all last night, and you've had this on top of it. I'm supposed to be doing an evening clinic, but there's still all your patients to see from this morning. And now we've got Joe who, if I'm not mistaken, is going to be darned hard work for the next few weeks.'

'We'll fly him out,' Blair said wearily. 'As soon as he looks like being stable we'll fly him to Perth. If his kidneys pack up then we can't cope.'

'OK, that's one thing off your plate, but there are more.' Rod's voice rose. From where Cari was standing she could hear every word. 'For heaven's sake, we've got a trained doctor who's out of a job. Why are we hesitating?'

'Because we don't know why she is out of a job.'

'So ask her.'

'Look, Rod, you know as much as I do. She's admitted her negligence killed someone and she's not saying any more. How can I employ her when that's all I know?'

'You use her for radio clinics.'

'That's different.' There was a pause, and Cari could imagine Blair running his hand through his dark hair in the gesture of fatigue she was beginning to know. 'Rex is behind her. He's on instructions not to leave her by herself. You know darn well that Rex could near run that clinic by himself. She's being watched every step of the way.'

'And this morning?'

'She's hardly likely to prove lazy and uncaring in a life-and-death situation,' Blair said bluntly. He hesitated. 'Look, Rod, I agree she seems competent—after this morning I'd have to say exceedingly competent. But she's been proved guilty of negligence, negligence that resulted in a death. That's all we know, and until we know any more, we can't take the risk.'

Cari fled.

Driving home, she thought about the overheard conversation. It hurt that she was viewed with such mistrust, even though she knew the mistrust was caused by her own reluctance to tell the truth. But if she did tell the truth?

She could do so and still see the mistrust in their eyes, she thought. And then the pain would be unbearable. She had told Harvey the truth. And she had told her family. All of them had responded with deepening disbelief and contempt.

Mistrust was with her from now on, she thought bitterly. She was just going to have to expect it. The only way she could avoid it was to avoid medicine entirely.

All of a sudden Slatey Creek started closing in on her. The sooner she got away from here the better. The sooner she got away from Blair Kinnane. . .

Why was Blair Kinnane's opinion of her so desperately important? Why did it hurt so much?

To her dismay she realised that she was crying. She brushed away the tears with anger. She'd done enough crying in the last twelve months to last a lifetime.

Jock came out to the veranda to meet her as she pulled up in front of the house five minutes later. Maggie was still at the hospital and he was eagerly awaiting news.

'Joe Craddock's a neighbour,' he explained briefly. 'He's a good man. It'd be a damned shame if we lost him.'

Cari nodded in agreement. Jock offered an arm to help her up the steps and she took it gratefully. Her whole body was aching.

'I've got some good news, though,' Jock told her as he closed the screen door after them. 'The insurance assessors have been through—they rang this morning. They said they'll either pay for your fare down to Perth to pick up a new car, or they can put a replacement vehicle on one of the trucks going through to the Alice. You should have it in ten days.'

Cari closed her eyes in relief. In ten days surely she would be well enough to start travelling. She could leave here. In ten days she need never see Blair Kinnane and Slatey Creek again.

And go where? Her tired mind asked the question.

It was too hard. It was enough, for now, that she could go.

CHAPTER EIGHT

CARI slept badly. Her body ached after its unaccustomed exertions, and the emotion of the day kept resurfacing in her tired mind. Towards dawn she fell into a fitful sleep, but the first rays of sun and the noises from the stirring household had her wide awake. She lay on her back with her hands under her head, watching the lazy whirring of the overhead fan.

There was a knock on the door and Maggie came in, bearing a cup of tea and hot buttered toast.

'Compliments of the management,' she smiled as Cari opened her mouth to protest. 'Jock's idea, and a darned good one. He brought me in some too, only a trifle earlier.'

'He must think we've been working,' Cari smiled.

'And so we have.' Maggie perched on the end of the bed and scrutinised Cari's face. 'Blair was right. It was too much.'

'What do you mean?' Cari pushed herself up on her pillows and gratefully accepted the steaming cup of tea.

'Three hours of solid standing in an operating theatre with associated tension is hardly the prescribed method of treatment for a broken pelvis,' Maggie retorted. 'Look at you! Your eyes are falling out of your head. Didn't you have enough sense to take some painkillers last night?'

Cari shook her head. 'I really don't need them any more,' she said firmly.

Maggie raised her eyebrows but didn't comment. 'Dr Kinnane has decreed that the hospital can manage

without your services this morning,' she continued. 'So
nestle down and have a sleep in, as per doctor's orders.
According to Blair, and according to me, you've earned
it.' Her voice was warm with admiration.

'Are they still busy in there?'

'I'd imagine so,' said Maggie. 'I'm not game to ring
in case they tell me to get on in there myself.'

Cari pushed back the covers and rose stiffly to her
feet.

'Then I'm going in.'

'Blair will have my hide! Cari, the man's worried
about you, and he has every reason to be.'

Cari turned and faced the worried woman sitting on
the bed. She spread her hands expressively.

'Maggie, Jock says my new truck can be here in ten
days. Although Blair may be concerned about me this
morning he's also told me that I owe a debt to the
Flying Doctor Service. He's right, and I've only ten
days left to repay that debt.'

'I'm sure Blair would say the debt's been paid in
full,' Maggie muttered.

Cari shook her head. 'I don't think, for Blair
Kinnane, my debt can ever be paid,' she said bleakly.

Blair met her in the hospital corridor as she arrived
for work. Normally he would have ignored her arrival,
but this morning he paused.

'I thought I told Maggie to keep you at home.'

Cari shook her head.

'I'm here to work,' she told him crisply. 'Make use
of me while you have the chance.'

'You're planning to leave soon?'

'In ten days,' she told him, ignoring the stab of pain
the words caused her. She looked up, trying to read
the expression in his eyes. It was undecipherable.

'I'm going out to Arlinga tomorrow,' he said curtly. 'Would you like to come?'

'Arlinga?'

'It's an Aboriginal camp about twenty kilometres from here. I'm just running a routine clinic. There's only about twenty-five people out there, so it shouldn't take long.' He paused. 'Maggie's saying that you'll be leaving here without an overall view of our work. She says it's not fair, and she's probably right. If you'd like to come you're welcome.'

His tone was about as welcoming as a douche of cold water. His words were inviting, but his eyes told her clearly that she should refuse.

Cari hesitated. Maggie was right in that she felt as if she was only seeing one tiny aspect of the Flying Doctor Service by being confined to the hospital.

'Would I get in the way?' Her tone was formal, to match his.

He shook his head. 'If I thought that, I wouldn't ask you. I usually take a sister, but you'll do instead.'

Cari knew enough of Blair Kinnane to know that, at least, to be true.

She looked up into his face. She still couldn't read his expression. The cool grey eyes gave nothing away. It was almost as if he was defying her to come, against his and against her better judgement. She took a deep breath.

'Thank you,' she said simply. 'I'd love to come.'

He nodded curtly and left her.

The next day dawned as had every other since Cari had arrived at Slatey Creek, hot and dry. Having been warned by Maggie, Cari dressed casually, in a soft, loose-fitting dress and open sandals.

'Don't wear make-up,' Maggie warned. 'It's murder

if the wind gets up and there's sand blowing. Just stick to a good sunscreen.'

Blair collected her after her morning radio clinic. They ate a light lunch in the hospital kitchen and then Cari helped checking equipment before they set up. Still the rigid formality was maintained. It was as if each was afraid of letting down the barriers.

Once they had left Slatey Creek behind them Blair loosened up slightly and described the country along the way. He made a good guide. It was as if he was now setting out to give her no cause for complaint about the information he was giving her.

Cari sat in the passenger-seat of the big four-wheel-drive van and relaxed while Blair expertly negotiated the rough track. After a while, faint wheel-marks where previous vehicles had turned off the main track appeared on their right, and Blair turned as well. They were now covering open country which didn't seem to be marked on any map.

As they went, he pointed out the things he found interesting. Cari listened, fascinated by his obvious love for this barren country as well as by the things he was telling her.

'There have been some pigs here lately,' he said suddenly. 'Look at those tracks.' In the soft sand the markings were unmistakable.

'Pigs?' Cari asked, startled. 'Are there native pigs here?'

Blair shook his head. 'Domestic animals gone wild and long time ago,' he said briefly. 'Now they're completely feral and a damned nuisance. They eat the stuff that the native animals and the station livestock need. The station owners kill them, but they breed up faster than we can cull them.'

Cari grimaced. Blair looked over and smiled slightly at her expression of distaste.

'You should get our Dr Daniels to talk about the pigs,' he continued, slowing the vehicle to negotiate a couple of sandy hummocks. 'He hates them.'

'Why?' It was the first time Blair's formal informative tone had slipped, and Cari held her breath.

He looked across at her consideringly. 'I'm not sure Rod would want me to tell it.' There was a gleam of humour in his eyes, and she responded with a smile.

'Go on,' she urged him.

'You won't tell Rod I've been spreading stories?'

Cari shook her head virtuously, and Blair laughed and relented.

'It was just after Rod arrived here,' he told her. 'He was driving out to a house call, along one of the roads near the Bromptons', and Maggie was driving towards him. She'd been off duty since Rod had arrived, so he didn't recognise her.'

'Go on,' Cari prompted. Blair grinned.

'They were both raising a huge cloud of dust behind them,' he continued, the smile staying in his eyes. 'There was only room on the track for one car. Rod was in a hurry and was darned if he was going to shift. He stuck to the track at full speed and forced Maggie off. As he passed her she put her head out the window and yelled, "Pig!"'

'And?' Cari was laughing already.

Blair fought for a straight face. 'Rod yelled a worse obscenity in reply. Fifty metres down the track he ran full tilt into the pig that Maggie was warning him about.'

'Oh, no!' Cari dissolved into a delighted peal of laughter. 'Poor Rod!'

'Poor Rod my foot,' Blair said firmly. 'He slunk back

into the hospital a couple of hours later, hoping he could pass his damaged car off as having hit a kangaroo, only to discover who the matron of the hospital was.'

Cari grinned. The tension between her and Blair had dissolved.

'You love this job and these people, don't you?' she said thoughtfully as the bubble of laughter within her subsided.

Blair nodded, his attention back on the sandy country they were negotiating.

'Why?'

There was a long silence. For a while Cari thought he wasn't going to reply. When he did, his words were slow and considered.

'I've tried to work that out.' He shook his head. 'I still don't have all the answers. I'm certainly not bred to it. I'm a city boy, born and bred.'

'Melbourne?' She already knew, but she wanted to hear it from him.

He nodded.

'You're a long way from home,' she remarked.

He looked over at her curiously. 'Not as far as you, Dr Eliss.'

Cari flushed. She stared at the loose knot her hands made in the soft folds of her dress before changing the subject back to Blair.

'So why choose to practise here?'

'I don't know.' He shook his head again. 'At a time when, for a couple of reasons, I was questioning what I was doing, an elderly doctor friend of my father's came to dinner one night when he was in Melbourne. It turned out he was the doctor at Slatey Creek and had been forced home because of ill health. He was worried sick about who was in charge up here, so I promised him I'd come and take a look. And I stayed.'

'Why?' Cari asked him again.

'I've told you—I don't know.' His hands tightened on the steering-wheel. 'I only know that it fills a need in me. The medicine I practise is honest. I get more than enough surgery to keep me happy and I find I still enjoy treating coughs and colds. Once you're in a specialty in the city you're completely divorced from that side of things. And the people here need and appreciate me.' He shrugged. 'What more can a man ask for?'

Cari looked over at the man beside her. His face was intent on the track ahead, his expression fixed as if it wasn't the sandy track that was endlessly before him but his whole life.

'You're running too,' she said softly.

Blair's hands gripped the steering-wheel. He flashed a look across at her of pure anger.

'Maggie's been talking.'

'Yes,' Cari agreed quietly.

For a while there was silence in the confines of the van.

'So what about you?' he asked suddenly, savagely. 'If you think I'm here because I'm running from personal relationships, then perhaps you're right. At least, that's what drove me here initially. But you. . . You're running from much more, aren't you, Dr Eliss?'

'What do you mean?'

'You can't keep running for ever,' Blair told her. 'The world's not a big enough place. Sooner or later, wherever you go, someone's going to find out what you've done.'

Cari stared at him. 'Is that what you think?' she asked finally. 'That I'm scared people will find out?'

'What else can I think?'

She gazed blankly at the man at her side. Her first reaction was anger and then, suddenly, weariness. It didn't matter what this man thought. In just over a week she would be gone. Let him think what he liked.

He was watching her, now, his eyes puzzled.

'Cari?'

'Yes?' It was an effort to get the word out.

'Am I wrong?'

'Go to hell!'

The scattered campsite of Arlinga broke the monotony of the desert before they could speak again. Cari stared ahead with relief. She needed to get out of this vehicle, to put some distance between Blair and herself.

As the vehicle pulled to a halt, the silence of tension became the silence of shock.

Arlinga. . . Cari had expected a miniature town, with buildings and facilities for a settlement of people. Here there was nothing but odd, makeshift humpies that sheltered the inhabitants from the sun and little else. Nothing.

Blair was obviously known and welcome. As the van pulled to a halt one of the older men came forward and greeted him formally. Once this was done it seemed the signal for the cluster of children in the camp to edge forward, examining the truck, Cari and Blair with an odd mixture of curiosity and shyness.

The van was set up for just such a situation. Swiftly Blair swung up the back of the van and pulled a canvas awning out to shade him and Cari while they worked. Tables and chairs followed, and before long there was a makeshift surgery ready for use.

Each of the children underwent an examination. Cari was content to assist Blair, handing him the instruments he needed as he worked and taking notes on his instructions.

'Ears need special attention out here,' he told her, examining those of a wide-eyed little boy of about four. 'Many if not most of the adults here have hearing loss associated with too many untreated ear infections.' He smiled at the child he was examining. 'Not that there's anything wrong with these.' He rumpled the little boy's hair. 'You're a fine, healthy boy. Now let's have a look at your little brother.'

The child backed off about a metre, stared at Blair for about ten seconds open-mouthed, then gave a huge infectious chuckle and ran away laughing.

The rest of the examinations went just as smoothly. 'We've been lucky,' Blair told Cari. 'It's not always as easy as this. Often a clinic will pick up infections that have been lingering for weeks.'

'Don't they come in for help?' she asked.

Blair shook his head. 'How?' He motioned around him. 'It's a bit far to walk if you're feeling unwell.'

'But can't they get a car?' she expostulated. 'Don't they have anything? They don't even seem to have a radio.' They were back in the van now, retracing their route.

'You think they should have?' asked Blair.

'Of course they should have some method of transport and communications,' Cari burst out. 'For heaven's sake, this is the twentieth century! And what about housing? Isn't there some sort of government assistance to find these people a place to live? What happens when it's raining or they're ill?'

Blair shook his head. 'To make comments like that means you don't know very much about these people,' he said wryly.

'What do you mean?'

'Simply that they don't want material possessions. To you a house and a car are important material possessions. To the Arlinga tribe they would be just things to enjoy while they felt like it and then to abandon when they no longer felt their need.'

'But that's crazy!'

'Is it?' asked Blair. 'It's a different point of view, and one which has developed over generation upon generation. These people have survived for thousands of years by sharing everything they had and by being free and unencumbered to move to wherever the food was. It's impossible to teach them greed in a generation or two.'

'Greed?' Cari queried.

He glanced across at her. 'Greed,' he repeated. 'Or just the concept of ownership. You don't have to call it greed if you don't want to, but the Aboriginals here will. The concept leaves them cold. You look at your average child's reactions to possessions. From an early age he's getting quite clear about the concept of "mine". The Aboriginal child seems to have no such concept.'

Cari shook her head in bewilderment as the ramifications of Blair's words sank in. 'You mean they don't want houses,' she said cautiously.

'They might,' he said. 'When it's cold and wet or when they're ill then they certainly would. But then the weather fines up or they become well again, and the house is useless. They move on.'

'Leaving the house behind?'

He raised his eyebrows in a question. 'Well, what else would they do with it?'

Cari sank into silence, trying to absorb Blair's words. Unlike their initial journey, their silence now was companionable, peaceful. She found herself wishing it didn't have to end. Not yet.

Their privacy was interrupted by a sound of static as the radio mounted on the dashboard sprang into life and Cari's wish was granted. Rex's voice sounded in the cabin.

'Doc?'

Blair picked up the handset.

'What is it, Rex?'

'I've had a call from Emily Spears. She says she's got tightness of breath and pain in her chest. Is it possible for you to come back via her place?'

Blair swore softly. He thought for a moment. 'It's going to bring me in after dark,' he said.

'I know,' said Rex. 'She sounds pretty concerned, though. I guess you could come in and take the plane back out, but it'd probably mean a night landing.'

Blair glanced appraisingly over at Cari.

'What's the problem?' she asked.

'Emily Spears lives about fifteen kilometres from here, as the crow flies. The track to her place is awful. We're going to risk being stuck there for the night.'

'Have we any choice?' she asked quietly.

'If I went fast back to Slatey Creek either Rod or I could take the plane out.'

'Which would involve a night landing,' Cari repeated.

He nodded. 'And Emily hasn't a landing-strip, and the road there is terrible.'

'Then we don't have a choice,' said Cari.

He nodded. 'I just thought I'd give you the option of out.'

So she couldn't complain later when she was stuck for the night. Cari bit her lip. Blair's opinion of her was plain.

'Let's go,' she said tightly. The possibility of having to spend the night on the road with Blair Kinnane made her heart sink, but there was no choice.

The Spearses place was a derelict house, surrounded by the debris of years. Old car bodies and rusted-out water tanks littered the yard. There was no greenery around the house at all and the fence keeping the livestock away from the house had long since fallen. It lay in a tangle of rusty wire and rotted wood.

As the van pulled up, a little nondescript dog jumped off the veranda, barking with what he obviously hoped was ferociousness. It didn't quite come off. For thirty seconds he stayed back from them, barking fiercely. As Blair reached down and clicked his fingers, he put his tail between his legs and rushed to greet them in a frenzy of welcome.

Blair and Cari picked their way cautiously across the junk to the house, the wiry little dog at their heels. Blair was moving swiftly. As he approached the veranda he broke into a run.

'Why the rush?' asked Cari, attempting to keep up with his stride. Her legs would not permit it, and she fell back.

'Emily should have heard us coming for the last five kilometres,' Blair responded curtly, without lessening his stride. 'She ought to be out on the veranda waiting for us.'

The reason why she wasn't was dreadfully obvious the moment they walked in the door. Emily was slumped in a chair, her body falling forward over the radio set on the bench in front of her. It took them only seconds to know that she was dead.

There was little to do. She was elderly and, according to Blair, had been suffering heart trouble for years. They took her body into the bedroom and laid it on the bed, covered her gently and closed the bedroom door.

'Why on earth was she living alone?' Cari asked in bewilderment. 'For an elderly lady with a heart condition to live here. . .' She shook her head.

'She wouldn't have it any other way,' Blair told her. 'Emily's husband died about five years back. She's got a daughter living in Perth who's been pleading with her to go to the city, but Emily was far more frightened of living in a city than of continuing here on her own. Besides. . .' he reached down and scooped up the little dog snuffling in bewilderment at their feet, 'she had Rusty.'

'What happens now?' The sadness of the place was enveloping Cari in depression.

'Nothing.' Blair glanced around the room they were in, moving to check that the windows were closed and secure. 'We'll contact her daughter tonight and I'll get the boys to collect the body and bring it in to Slatey Creek tomorrow. There's nothing more we can do.'

'And the dog?' Cari looked anxiously at the little dog and then up to find Blair regarding her curiously.

'You're not great at professional detachment, Dr Eliss.'

Cari flushed and was silent. Blair looked down at the disreputable animal in his arms. Rusty's ears fell forward, three-quarters covering his large, dark eyes. The eyes were gazing anxiously up at Blair, as if the little dog sensed that this man held the key to his future.

'I guess his fate will be up to Emily's daughter,' he said gently.

'Tonight, I mean?' Cari was looking at him with an expression almost as anxious as the little dog's, and, despite the gravity of the situation, Blair burst out laughing. He handed the little animal into her out-stretched hands.

'It looks like he's going to get a ride into Slatey Creek tonight,' he said resignedly. He looked at the pair of them and suddenly reached out and touched Cari lightly on the cheek. 'What a pair of waifs!' He glanced at his watch. 'At least we can travel part of the way in. It's getting late and it's nearly a two-hour trip from here.'

'We won't make it?'

Blair shook his head. 'We could if it was absolutely necessary, but it's taking the same sort of risks that you took, and look where it landed you. If I get an urgent message that I'm needed then I'll go in.'

'You mean you want to stay here?' Cari could think of nothing worse than spending the night in this bleak house that death had so recently touched.

He shook his head, his eyes reflecting understanding of her thoughts.

'We'll get about an hour's travelling done before dusk,' he said. 'We've got equipment in the van for rough camping. That way we've only another hour's travelling to cover at dawn.'

Cari nodded, relieved. The thought of camping on the roadside with Blair left her cold, but the thought of staying where they were was a thousand times worse.

CHAPTER NINE

As THEY left the farm Blair radioed Slatey Creek and told Rex what was happening. An hour later, as the dusk became dark, they pulled off the track near a rocky outcrop which Blair obviously knew.

'It gives us a bit of protection from the wind,' he explained. He backed the van in to the rock face, and, by the light of a big gas lantern, pulled out the canopy.

'Home,' he announced.

Cari regarded it dubiously. 'It doesn't look like any home I've ever lived in,' she retorted. 'What happens if it rains?'

'We sleep in the van or we get wet,' Blair said blandly. He looked upward at the darkening sky, already showing promise of a cloudless, star-filled night. 'I'd say our chances of rain tonight are about five thousand to one.'

Cari nodded. She stood and watched Blair make the preparations for the evening, feeling inept that there was little she could do to help. At her feet Rusty made half-hearted attempts to sniff this new territory, but his heart wasn't in it. In the end Cari sat and took the confused little dog on to her lap. He heaved a huge sigh and lay dolefully in her arms. She looked down at him with sympathy. He seemed just as lost and confused as. . .as she was.

She acknowledged the truth of her unwelcome thoughts. She too was without roots, not knowing what the next day would hold. At least she could have some say in her own future. The woebegone little dog in her arms was totally at the mercy of these strange humans who had removed him from his Emily. Cari's arms tightened on the little creature and she gently stroked his ear.

'Dinner's ready.'

She looked up in surprise. Blair was kneeling in front of the Primus, spooning something from a saucepan on to two plates. Cari approached with interest.

'That was fast!' she remarked.

'World's speediest cook!' he agreed gravely. Cari took the proffered plate and burst into laughter.

'Baked beans!'

'What were you expecting?' he demanded in a wounded voice. 'Oysters Kilpatrick followed by a steak with béarnaise sauce?'

'It would have been nice,' Cari grinned.

'Shut up and eat, woman,' he growled, his smile making a mockery of his ferocity.

In the end, she enjoyed the simple meal. She had been hungry, she thought. She offered some to Rusty, but he sniffed uninterestedly. His world had been too severely shaken for him to retain his appetite.

Afterwards Blair boiled a billy and they drank tea from big enamel mugs.

Cari was quiet and self-conscious, increasingly aware of their isolation and the presence of this man beside her. As the evening progressed, Blair too fell silent. It was as if every word between them was charged with something intangible.

Blair produced air-beds and sleeping-bags from the recesses of the truck.

'What else have you got in there?' Cari laughed.

'We have to be prepared. There's a bit of a dearth of motels in these parts.'

They set the beds up under the canopy. Rusty settled

immediately on the foot of Cari's sleeping-bag. She didn't shift him. She was beginning to think she needed the little dog's presence as much as he needed her. As Blair started to pull off his shirt and trousers she turned deliberately away and slid swiftly out of her loose cotton dress. Underneath she wore only a scanty pair of briefs. They were staying on. She slid quickly into the relative security of her sleeping-bag.

The man beside her was too close for her to relax; the air-beds were separated by millimetres.

The night was calm and still. Rusty stirred, whined softly and settled again. The silence around them was absolute.

'Cari?' Blair's voice came out of the dark.

'Yes?'

'Will you tell me what happened?'

Cari's body froze. 'What do you mean?'

'You know what I mean,' he said quietly. 'What happened back in the United States? Why are you running?'

'I'm not running.'

There was a long silence. Cari stirred restlessly in her bag. At her feet, Rusty whimpered in protest.

'Why do you need to know?' she asked at last. Her voice was bitter, laced with pain. 'It's got nothing to do with you. What right have you got to interrogate me?'

Blair raised himself on his elbow and looked down at her pale face in the moonlight.

'I need to know,' he said simply.

'Why?' Cari turned her face away from his searching eyes.

'Because. . .' His voice faded into nothing and he lay back, as if he too was confused by the undercurrent of emotions between them.

'You've no right to question me,' she said angrily.

'You're running too, remember? If your marriage had been happy there's no way you'd be here now, devoting yourself to outback medicine.'

'Is that why you think I'm staying?'

'Because you're afraid of relationships? Because here you can always call the tune? You don't have to get involved. You don't have to risk being hurt.'

Cari paused, almost gasping in shock at what she had said. She had no right to throw these accusations at Blair Kinnane. She had no right. All she had was the desire to hurt, the desire to throw back some of the trauma she was suffering on to someone else. She wanted to make Blair hurt like she was hurting.

The silence stretched endlessly. Cari found she was hardly breathing, overcome by the enormity of what she had said.

Finally Blair swore savagely and sat up. He turned to grasp her by the shoulders, hauling her up to face him. The soft folds of the sleeping-bag slid away, leaving her naked to the waist. She grabbed frantically to cover herself, but his hands were shaking her savagely.

'What the hell do you know, Cari Eliss? Who the hell are you to talk about being afraid? You've left your country to get away from people and situations you haven't the courage to face, and you can still find it in you to criticise me for being afraid to commit myself!'

Cari pulled back, but his grip was ruthless, his words hard and cruel.

'I don't know what the hell you've done that you're so ashamed of, or what you're running from. Where are you going to get, Dr Eliss, with all this running? There's nowhere smaller than Slatey Creek. There's nowhere further away. And still you're running.'

'I'm not running!' It was a cry of pain.

His hands still gripped her shoulders. The feel of his touch was sending fire through her. At her waist lay the edges of her sleeping-bag, forgotten. Her taut breasts stood out white against the blackness around them.

'You are running,' he said harshly, his fingers digging into the softness of her skin. 'And from what? From medicine? Or from me?'

The words were out. They hung in the stillness between them, almost as a taunt, endlessly mocking.

'It's you who's running from relationships,' Cari whispered. 'It's you who's afraid.'

'And you're not.'

'No,' she choked. And then she drew a breath and found strength to raise her voice. 'Why should I be afraid of a man who won't let women near him, who's so damned frightened of losing his independence he holds women in contempt? Why should I be frightened of you, Blair Kinnane?'

'Shut up!' His voice was a tight hard command.

'Why should I shut up?' Her control had broken. The anger and hurt of the last few months crashed around her, and all she wanted to do was to hurt him as much as possible, to make his eyes reflect her pain. She glared up at him, defying him to fresh anger. 'Why should I——?'

'Shut up!'

'I——'

His mouth came down on hers.

It was a savage kiss, devoid of any tenderness, a punishing, brutal meeting of flesh. Cari pulled back in shock, but his hold was implacable. She was no match for his strength.

She fought like a wildcat, beating her hands against

his naked chest, trying frantically to break his hold. It was useless. Finally her struggle weakened and died. Somewhere deep inside her a fire caught hold, spreading upward and outward from her body into the man holding her tightly against him.

Suddenly she was released. She fell back, gasping with shock. Her fingers went up to touch her bruised lips. Her eyes didn't leave Blair's face.

'Leave me be,' she managed to say. Her voice was a ragged sob.

'Cari. . .' It was a whisper of wonder, of shock. Blair pulled back, holding her at arm's length. 'Cari?'

In the soft rays of the moon his gaze held hers, searching her face for some answer to his unspoken question. Cari's eyes reflected his confusion, and reflected his desire. Somewhere between them the anger dissipated as if it had never been, rising to disappear in the star-filled outback sky. With a groan he sank back to meet the soft, sweet mouth.

His tongue gently probed her lips, searching for an entry. As Cari's lips parted involuntarily she felt his tongue enter her, exploring her teeth, her tongue, the moist recesses of her mouth.

Her body no longer belonged to her. Anger, loneliness, distrust, all were forgotten. Deep within the growing fire was consuming her. Its core was deep, deep between her thighs, stirring the rest of her body and taking control from her brain.

Her hands came up to hold Blair's face to her. Her fingers felt the roughness of his unshaven cheeks, and she gloried in the masculinity of their feel. Slowly her hands dropped to the bare skin of his chest, moving tentatively, joyfully through the wiry hairs running down to his navel. There wasn't an ounce of fat on his hard, demanding body.

Blair's tongue stopped its searching, and as it left her mouth Cari felt her own come out to make an exploration of its own. His lips were hard, possessing. Behind them she tasted the salt of his mouth, the taste of Blair Kinnane. For him too the anger and hurt she had inflicted seemed as if they were forgotten. He was holding her, caressing her as if he loved her.

As if he loved her. . .

Her brain responded to the inadvertent thought, and for a moment she responded with pure fright. She pulled away, her eyes wide.

Blair felt her resistance, and let her move. She sat up and backed frantically.

'What's wrong, Cari?'

'I. . . I don't want this.' Suddenly she had gone far enough. Perhaps she could cope with the fact that she loved, that she was hopelessly in love with Blair, but if she let herself believe that Blair could return that love—and if once again her house of cards came crumbling round her. . .

She couldn't bear it. She couldn't bear to expose herself again to hurt and humiliation. Perhaps even now he was thinking that she also was one of the tough ones, one like Liz who took love for what it could give them.

'I don't want this,' she repeated desperately.

'Yes, you do.' His voice was suddenly full of laughter.

'I don't!' She was almost weeping.

'Why not?' The laughter was receding, to be replaced by a mixture of tenderness and understanding. This man saw too much, Cari thought bitterly. Could he see how much she wanted him?

'Why not?' he asked again. He reached out and laid a finger on her shoulder. She was bare from the waist up. He ran the finger down lightly along the contour of her breast, to touch the proudly upstanding nipple. 'Your body doesn't say not,' he smiled. And then he moved her hand down gently to touch him. 'And despite the very grave reservations I have,' he said, half mockingly, 'my body doesn't say not.'

'We haven't. . .we haven't taken any precautions,' Cari said desperately.

Blair's gentle smile deepened. 'I can fix that,' he said softly. He stood up and walked around to the front of the van. In a moment he was back. 'All fixed,' he told her.

'Very convenient,' Cari said harshly. 'Do you have those ready for when you bring Sister McKinley along?'

Blair's smile slipped. He sank down on to his knees and took her face between his hands.

'Dr Eliss,' he said firmly, 'for a bright lady, you can sometimes be very stupid.'

'Don't you make love to her? Isn't this just more of the same?' Cari's voice was shrill with accusation, but she didn't care. She was out of control. 'Am I just someone to fill a need because you can't bear the thought of another wife?'

His eyes darkened with anger. He drew back and for a moment she thought he was going to strike. And then something of her fear must have broken through, some vestige of the fact that this too was another defence. Slowly the anger died.

'I have not slept with a woman since I left my wife,' he said dispassionately. 'Is that what you needed to know, Cari? Or would you rather believe the worst of me? It would be much more convenient, I agree.'

She glared up at him. The dark eyes watched her, unmoving. Slowly her glare faded, to be replaced by uncertainty. Her feeble defences were shattered by this man she loved, this man she wanted with all her heart.

She put a finger out and traced the course of his cheekbones. Still his eyes didn't leave her face. The loneliness and fear of the last twelve months welled up within her, to be replaced by the knowledge that, for tonight at least, it had come to an end.

'Blair?' Her voice was a thread in the silence around them.

His eyes queried her.

'I'm sorry.'

He nodded, running a hand along the silken tresses of her hair. Her body trembled at his touch, aching with desire.

'And Blair?'

His smile had returned, and his grey eyes warmed her heart.

'Take me,' she said.

There was nothing more to be said. Blair opened his sleeping-bag out to become a soft, welcoming blanket. Cari was lifted from her air-bed and her body lowered gently on to the soft folds. Somehow her wisp of underwear disappeared. For a moment Blair stood above her, savouring the beauty of her waiting body. Then, as she reached up to pull him down to her, he sank to gather her into him. In the stillness of the night, under the starlit night sky of the desert, they became one.

Cari woke as dawn broke. The sun was a soft, warm glow on the horizon. At some stage in the night—she couldn't remember when—Blair had opened the other bag and had laid it across them. She was languorously warm and content.

Blair's arms were still around her, possessive, exultant even in sleep. She thought lazily back to the night before, and pleasure at the memory engulfed her once again. She and Harvey had made love, but it had never been like this. Harvey had seemed to find satisfaction, but with Cari it was always as if there was something missing. That something she had found last night.

She stirred contentedly. Beside her, Blair opened his eyes, then his arms tightened around her naked body.

'Going somewhere?' he murmured sleepily. He swept her hair from her shoulder and kissed the soft skin behind her ear.

'Shouldn't we be going?' she asked. She fought to get her wrist free. 'It's five-thirty.'

'There's time enough,' Blair whispered, his voice husky with passion.

'For what?' she asked, laughter in her voice.

He pushed himself up on an elbow and looked at her consideringly.

'Well, let me see.' He leaned forward and kissed the hollow at the base of her neck. Then he turned his attention to the rising mounds of her breasts, cupping each one in turn and lightly kissing the taut nipple. 'We really don't have to leave here for another hour or so. Can you think of some way we could fill in the time?' His words were interspersed with featherlike kisses.

'We could have breakfast.' Cari's voice was light with love and laughter.

'Mmm,' he agreed. His mouth was at the indentation of her navel, his tongue exploring its recesses. 'That'll take ten minutes.' His voice was slurred. 'That leaves fifty minutes. Next suggestion?'

'We could take the dog for a walk.'

Blair shifted his attention for a brief moment. 'It looks as if Rusty has taken himself for a walk.' His head lowered again. 'Next suggestion?'

Cari gasped as she realised where his exploration was taking him. Blair looked up wickedly and laughed. 'All out of ideas, Dr Eliss?'

'I'm lost for words,' she said breathlessly. She lay back, letting waves of pleasure sweep over her. This man could do anything he liked to her. Until this moment she didn't know that such pleasure could exist.

'Oh, Blair. . . Oh. . .'

'Cari?'

He left what he was doing and rose to meet her. Her hands reached out to hold him fiercely to her. They met, skin against skin, the warmth of contact running the full length of their bodies.

As if of one accord they broke away, each seeking to search the other's eyes. For a long moment they lay unmoving, making love with their eyes. Somewhere Blair's deep reserve had disappeared as if it had never been. His eyes told her that she was loved.

Then the physical need became unbearable. With a cry of triumph he raised her above him and brought her down hard against him. She felt him come into her and the dawn faded again into a myriad stars.

Afterwards they lay, too sated to speak. Words were superfluous. Cari was lost in a whirl of love and desire. At some inner level she knew that what she was experiencing couldn't last. Somehow things would be snatched away from her again as they had been in the past. If she lay quite still and didn't move, perhaps this peak of joy could stretch out, stretch out. . .

'We have to go.' Blair's voice was slurred with contentment. Cari's wrist was lying across his chest, and he lifted it lightly and grimaced. 'We've managed to fill in fifty minutes quite nicely, Dr Eliss. And some,' he added ruefully. 'Next on the list is breakfast and Slatey Creek.'

'I don't want to go,' Cari said sleepily.

He rose and stood looking down at her, then reaching down, he grasped her wrists and pulled her up to stand against him.

'The future has to be faced,' he said lightly. He bent and kissed her.

The trip in to Slatey Creek was done mostly in silence. Everything was too new, too recent to find expression in words. Cari sat with the little dog on her lap, watching the vast sandy plains unfold around them. It seemed unreal, as if this was happening in some misty and pleasurable dream. Any moment now she would wake up.

'Are you going to tell me about it now?' Blair asked gently.

The dreamlike quality faded, and Cari shivered involuntarily as the chill of reality hit home.

'Why I'm running away?' she asked quietly

'Why you're running away.'

Cari was silent. Blair looked across at her, lifted a hand from the steering-wheel and ran a finger gently down her cheek.

'It can't make it any worse,' he said lightly.

It could. Cari cringed inwardly at the thought of relating the events of the last few months. She remembered her words during the court case and the polite disbelief of the judge and jury. To tell Blair. . .to see him turn away as Harvey had done before. . .

Let him think what he liked. He could have the version that everyone else believed. To explain was to expose herself again to disbelief and ridicule. The thought was more than she could bear.

'There's nothing to tell other than what you already know,' she said dully. 'My negligence killed a child. I was successfully sued and I came here. End of story.'

'So tell me about it,' he insisted.

Cari shook her head.

'Tell me.' His voice was harsh and insistent, echoing back and forth in the little cabin. She took a deep breath.

'All right, if it means so much to you.' She swallowed painfully, trying to force the difficult words out. 'I failed to notice a loose connection while ventilating a patient—a little girl. By the time my boss took over and noticed what I'd done it was too late. She died a couple of days later.'

There was a deep silence. Cari concentrated on a knot in Rusty's fur, fixing her vision so she could see nothing else. Blair stared straight ahead.

'I don't believe it,' he said at last.

'If you don't you'll be the only one who doesn't,' Cari said harshly. 'The judge, the jury and the hospital administration all believed it. Go ahead,' she goaded, 'prove them wrong.'

He frowned in concentration. 'To fail to notice. . . For that amount of damage to have been done the child would have been blue. Blue for a long time too.' He hesitated 'So why weren't you de-registered if you were so blatantly negligent?'

Cari closed her eyes. 'Do you mind?' she said wearily 'I've told you all you have to know. Now let's leave it.'

'Cari. . .'

'Please,' she pleaded, 'leave it alone.' The pain welled up in her. 'Leave me alone!'

'Do you mean that?'

'Yes!' Her word was an anguished cry. 'Yes, I do. I don't want your probing, Blair. I don't want. . .'

'You don't want me?'

She jerked her head up and stared across at him. What had he said? All of a sudden his face looked vulnerable, as if he too was afraid.

It didn't matter. It couldn't matter. Whatever he was offering, she wasn't free to take it. For all the joy that she had felt last night, there was no future here. Blair Kinnane meant personal commitment and medicine. Neither of those she was free to take. Both left her wide open, exposed to the same disasters she had fled from.

'No,' she said bleakly, 'I don't want you.'

CHAPTER TEN

THE next few days passed in a haze of misery. Cari avoided Blair as if, by not seeing him, she could somehow block out his existence.

She had been crazy to give in to him, she told herself. She had been crazy to give in to the wishes of her heart and the instincts of her body. She had been unhappy before. Now. . .

Her one solace out of the mess she had put herself in was the little dog. She took Rusty out to the Bromptons' farm with some trepidation.

'It's only until Emily's daugher arrives from Perth,' she explained anxiously, and Maggie burst into delighted laughter.

'You goose! Do you seriously think we'd be put out because of one more dog?' She looked down fondly at her pack of assorted canines, each vying to be the first to investigate the new addition to the household. 'This one's so small he won't even increase the food bill. If Emily's daughter doesn't want him, he's welcome to stay.'

Cari smiled with relief. Whatever happened now, Rusty would be secure as one of the Bromptons' pack.

Rusty, however, had other ideas. He associated politely with the other dogs, and greeted Maggie, Jock and the children with friendliness. He made it quite clear, however, that he was now Cari's dog.

On the first night they were back at the farm Cari put him out with the other dogs. Just as she was drifting off to sleep, however, there was a faint whining at her window. When she rose and opened the screen the little dog launched himself at her, wiggling all over in its excitement at finding her.

'I suppose you think you're clever,' Cari said severely.

Rusty aimed his tongue at her face and took a swipe.

'Ugh!' She wiped her face and put the little dog on the floor. 'The place for dogs is outside,' she said firmly.

Two big brown eyes peered up at her from under the disreputable ears.

'I don't hold with pets inside. It's unhygienic.'

Rusty's expression changed to one of personal affront, and Cari laughed. 'All right,' she conceded. 'Just not on my bed, OK?'

In the end Rusty compromised by sleeping on the floor as close to her head as he could. Cari found herself dozing off with her hand nestled in the little dog's fur. Just who was comforting whom? she thought ruefully.

Finally she took delivery of her truck. It was an almost exact replica of the one she had destroyed. Jock drove her in to take delivery and she drove it back to the farm, Rusty sitting proudly on the seat beside her.

There was now no reason for Cari to stay. She glanced down at the little dog and bit her lip. 'I don't know what I'm going to do with you,' she said ruefully. 'You're going to have to stay with the Bromptons.' Emily's daughter had made it quite clear that she didn't want anything to do with him; in fact her instructions as to what should be done with Rusty had left Cari feeling ill.

Rusty sank on to her lap and looked up at her.

'Well, what else can I do?' she demanded. 'I can hardly take you back to the States.'

She was going to have to return. She knew that now. A tiny voice was telling her with absolute certainty that she now had another reason to run. She needed to put as much distance between Blair Kinnane and herself as she could.

'I'll tell you what,' said Maggie, when Cari presented her with her dilemma. She had come into Cari's bedroom and was watching as Cari attempted to sort some order into her belongings. 'Why don't you take Rusty with you until you run out of travelling here in Australia? When you leave for the States, put him on a plane and send him back to us.'

'Would he get here all right?'

Maggie nodded. 'As long as the airlines are informed of what they're carrying he'll be treated royally,' she assured her. She eyed Cari more closely. 'Cari, why the rush? You know that your pelvis isn't properly healed. Jock and I are really enjoying the company, so why do you have to leave?'

Cari bit her lip and looked away. 'I just have to,' she said quietly. 'I can't stay here any longer.'

'Because of Blair Kinnane?'

Cari looked up, startled. 'I. . . How did you guess?'

Maggie smiled sympathetically. 'It's not hard when you know the signs,' she said. 'I've fallen hard myself.'

'With Jock?'

'Well, who else?' Maggie demanded with asperity, and Cari dredged up a laugh.

'You were lucky, though,' she sighed. 'You fell in love with someone who was free to love you, and you were free to love him.'

'So why are you and Blair different?' Maggie demanded.

'Blair loved his wife. I don't think he's free to love anyone else.'

Maggie snapped her fingers. 'That for his wife,' she said crudely. 'It seems to me that he's been treating his wife as an ever-present ghost for years now, blocking him from rebuilding his life. It's my belief that Blair Kinnane's available for the catching. More than available.'

'You make it sound as if he were a fish!' Cari protested, half laughing.

'Well. . .' Maggie said consideringly, then laughed with Cari, 'Perhaps not.' Her face grew serious again. 'What about you, Cari? You talk as if you're not free as well.' She glanced down at Cari's left hand and drew it up towards her. Since teenage years Cari had worn Harvey's ring, and a faint mark still lay around the third finger of her left hand. 'You're not married, are you?' Maggie asked, startled.

Cari shook her head. 'I was engaged before I left the States,' she said.

'And you're still hurting?'

'Let's just say I'm still carrying the scars,' Cari replied.

She pulled her battered suitcase from the top of the wardrobe and continued the methodical packing. For a while Maggie stayed, until she was sure that Cari didn't wish to talk. Then she left her to it.

The next morning was supposed to be Cari's last day on radio clinic. She had made a habit of parking around the back of the hospital and entering through the hospital kitchens. That way she ran less chance of encountering Blair doing his ward rounds. Her routine must have been noted, however, because Rod was sitting at one of the big preparation tables, drinking coffee and clearly lying in wait for her.

'The kettle's hot,' he said briefly. 'I need to talk to you, Cari. Will you have a coffee?'

Cari glanced at her watch. There was still half an hour to go before she was needed. She looked at Rod curiously. His usual easygoing good humour had slipped. His face was tense and strained. She nodded and sat down, waiting while he busied himself getting her coffee. As he placed it in front of her she saw, with a shock, that he was having trouble keeping back tears.

'Has something happened?' she said gently.

He nodded. 'My father.' Rod was speaking with difficulty, holding his coffee-cup with trembling fingers. Cari reached out and laid a hand on his.

'Is he dead?' she asked.

Her shock tactics worked. He looked sharply up at her and took a deep breath before shaking his head.

'No,' he said finally. 'Sorry, Cari. I've only just had the phone call, and it's knocked me sideways, I don't mind admitting.'

'So what is it?'

'He's had a stroke—they don't know yet how serious, but it looks bad.' He looked up at her. 'Cari, I'm their only son. My mom's by herself. I have to go.'

Cari nodded. 'Of course.'

He looked pleadingly at her. 'I can't leave Blair, though,' he continued. 'If I leave, Blair can do nothing. He can't even do emergency surgery. He can't do house calls. He'd be restricted to his surgery here and the radio clinics you've been doing.' Rod closed his eyes and continued in a voice drained of emotion, 'If that has to happen, then I can't go. My leaving would be killing patients here, and I can't do that. I've never taken this job really seriously, but I did give Blair a commitment that I'd stay out my term. I'll stick to it if I have to.'

'So you want me to stay.' Cari had seen it coming.

'Could you?' He looked up, his face a mute appeal, and she was reminded suddenly of Rusty and his floppy-eared, big-eyed pleading. Both were impossible to deny.

'Rod, even if I said yes I don't know how Blair will accept that.'

'Blair will accept it.' The voice from behind them made Cari swing around. Unnoticed, Blair had come up behind them. Cari flushed, then met his gaze challengingly.

'I'm a negligent doctor, remember?' she said bitterly. 'What use would I be to you?'

'Rod needs to go home,' Blair said firmly, 'If you're prepared to work I'm prepared to have you on the staff.'

'How are you going to keep tabs on me when there's only you and me?' Cari demanded.

'I trust you.'

She laughed.

'It's true.'

'Tell me, then,' she asked softly, 'why does Rex never leave the room when I'm doing radio clinic?'

'I have no idea.'

Cari raised her eyebrows. 'You mean, you didn't give him explicit instructions to keep an ear on what I was doing?' she continued.

Silence. Cari's angry eyes met Blair's, then fell away. The silence stretched on and on.

Blair swore explosively. He turned away from the table and strode to the window. With his hands gripping the sill and his gaze out over the dusty paddocks behind the hospital he continued, 'Cari, you've told us bluntly enough that your negligence killed a child. Can I, as a doctor responsible for the patients in this area, overlook that fact?'

'But you'll have to because you're desperate?'

'Yes.'

'So a negligent doctor is better than no doctor at all,' she said shortly. 'Well, well, perhaps I've a career left after all.'

Rod stood up. 'Look,' he said tiredly, 'perhaps I'd better stay. I can't see any way out of this.'

'I can't either,' said Cari. 'I'm sorry, Rod.' She turned and left the room.

By the end of her radio clinic the events of the morning were churning over and over in her mind. Rod's pleading eyes kept rising and haunting her. She knew she could give good service to this town while he was away. If she had to accept and live with Blair's mistrust while she gave it, then perhaps she would just have to find the courage to do it.

She would also be thrust in his way, over and over again. She shrugged to herself decisively. There was too much on her conscience already, depriving Rod of visiting his father was not something she was willing to add to the list. As the last patient signed out, she rose stiffly from her chair and went to find Blair.

He was in the hospital clinic. Cari waited for him to finish with the elderly man whose leg he was dressing, then went in, closing the door after her.

He looked up as she entered.

'How will you organise things if I stay?' she asked him bluntly.

Blair rose from his desk where he had been filling in a history and came towards her. He put his hands on her shoulders and looked down at her.

'Cari, what is this?'

'I don't know what you mean,' she said defensively.

He sighed. 'Well, it's about time you did,' he said harshly. 'You tell me you committed an unforgivable medical act of negligence and you refuse to give me any details. Then you act as if you're personally affronted because I can't, in conscience, give you any responsibility.'

Cari was silent.

'So tell me,' he repeated.

She shook her head. Couldn't this man understand that the time for explanation was over? The image of the judge and the people in the courtroom rose over and over in her mind. There were also the senior medical people in the hospital where she worked. She had told them and told them. No matter what her words were, or what the truth was, the version was set, unalterable. In the end it was better that things were left. What had the hospital administrator said? 'If you admit you made a mistake then you can start again, Cari. If you continue in this vein you'll be labelled a liar as well as incompetent.'

There was nothing that Cari could change. The massive pay-out from her medical insurance had been the final seal on her guilt. Now she only had to learn to live with the shame and disgust of the people around her.

And Blair Kinnane? At the moment he too thought she had made a mistake, a dreadful one, but, as the administrator had said, a mistake that could somehow, in time, be forgiven and lived down. If she attempted to explain to him. . . To be branded a liar by Blair Kinnane was more than she could bear.

She shook her head. 'There's nothing to tell,' she said wearily. 'I did a dreadful thing, and I'm paying and paying. It means I'm no longer happy practising medicine. Rod needs to go home, though, and I'm willing to put aside my unwillingness and cover for him for the time that he's away. It would involve you accepting that my mistake taught me a deep and dreadful lesson that I'm not about to commit again.'

'But how the hell did it happen in the first place?'

'I told you,' Cari said dully. 'Pure negligence on my part. Now are you willing to accept me on those terms or not?'

He looked at her for a long moment. 'It seems I haven't a choice,' he said.

Cari nodded. 'That goes for both of us.' She made to turn away, but Blair gripped her shoulders more firmly, forcing her to meet his eyes.

'Cari, this thing between us——'

'Is over,' she said harshly. 'It should never have started in the first place. I was a fool.'

'To want me?'

'To think I could ever rebuild anything out of this mess,' she said wearily. 'Blair, I don't need or want emotional entanglements, and if you're honest with yourself you could never be happy knowing what I've done in the past. You're too much of a perfectionist. The great Blair Kinnane has made one ghastly mistake in his life. He doesn't want another one.' Her voice was bitter.

'Cari, that's not fair.'

'Isn't it?' She laughed humourlessly. 'Perhaps you're right. My sense of fair play has been missing for a long time now.' She put her hands up and pushed away from his hold. 'The kindest thing you can do for me, Dr Kinnane, is leave me alone. I don't want you. I don't need anyone.'

Blair shook his head. 'Cari, you're wrong,' he said

quietly. 'You need me more than I need you.' He stood back, watching her gravely. 'And I'm beginning to think that, despite what you've done, I need you almost as I need a part of me.'

Despite what you've done. . . The words hung between them in the heavy silence.

'No,' Cari said harshly. 'I'm not committing myself again. I don't want any more pain. I've had enough to last a lifetime, and I don't need any more.'

'Would my love cause you pain?'

'Yes!' She practically yelled the word. Images of her father, her brothers, Harvey, crowded in, mocking her with their faces of disgust and disdain. All the people she thought she had loved, who she thought loved her. . . Not again.

'Leave me alone, Blair Kinnane,' she said savagely. 'I'm here for the next few weeks to work, but if you come near me, so help me, I'll walk out of here and leave you with no one. I have no choice.'

She turned and walked swiftly down the corridor. She didn't look back.

After twenty minutes standing in the little staff-room trying to regain some composure, Cari went to find Rod.

'You're free to go,' she told him.

The look on his face was almost worth the effort the interview with Blair had cost her. 'How soon can you fly out?' she asked him.

'There's a plane from Alice this afternoon,' Rod said exultantly. 'I can get them to touch down here and pick me up, and I can be on a direct flight from Perth home tonight.'

Cari smiled. For Rod, at least it would be fast, even

though it meant her work-load would start this afternoon.

'Are you sure?' Rod asked anxiously.

She nodded. 'I've talked to Blair,' she said. 'We can work out a way of coping. There's nothing for you to worry about. Just go home and give your full attention to your family. I hope by the time you get there your dad is so well you'll have wasted your time going.'

Rod smiled ruefully. 'I hope so too,' he said. 'I'll be back on the next plane if he is.'

'Don't be silly,' Cari said firmly. 'I'm here for a month. Have a break and spend some time with your dad.' She didn't say what they both knew, that once an elderly man had suffered one stroke, no matter how completely he recovered, there was no guarantee that another one wouldn't occur shortly afterwards.

Rod nodded. He leaned forward and kissed her lightly. 'Thank you,' he said simply.

'It's my pleasure.' It was almost true. The remembered lightness in Rod's face would be a source of real pleasure.

'Is there anything I can do for you while I'm home?' asked Rod. 'I've a host of cousins in California and the family tends to go back and forth a lot. Anything you want taken home or brought back?'

Cari shook her head.

'Where did you practise?' Rod asked. He was starting to sort his desk into order as he spoke.

'Los Angeles.'

'Which hospital?'

'Chandler.' Cari's voice was tight, but Rod didn't seem to notice. He nodded.

'That's one of the bigger private places,' he said meditatively. 'I've a feeling one of my cousins works there. He's a surgeon—Ed Daniels. Do you know him?'

Cari shook her head in relief.

'It was in one of my mother's letters a few months back,' Rod continued. 'He'd only just started there then, so I guess it'd be after your time.' He abandoned the discussion, pulled open the diary he'd just retrieved from the pile of paperwork on top of his desk and pointed to the first entry for the afternoon. 'OK, Dr Eliss, let's put you to work.'

CHAPTER ELEVEN

THE ensuing weeks were the hardest Cari had ever known. There was enough work at Slatey Creek for four doctors. Between them, she and Blair managed, but every time she lifted her head there was another job waiting.

The issue of trust receded. There was simply too much work to be done for Blair to be constantly watching, and after a week of solid work Cari knew she was not being observed. She was practising on her own.

The realisation brought with it a sense of relief that surprised even her. To practise medicine again, to be busy and needed, was a joy in itself.

The pain of losing her medical skills was still there, waiting to descend again as soon as she again became idle, but for the next month she could operate without it fogging her mind and dulling her brain.

She couldn't avoid Blair. With him she was required to work as a team, and twenty times a day they met, to operate, to discuss patients and to organise the allocation of duties. From the start Blair treated her with formality, and Cari responded with the same.

The formality even extended to their addressing each other as Dr Kinnane and Dr Eliss. It was stilted and difficult, but Cari found that it was her only means of blotting out her emotional reaction to the man she worked with. Whether Blair felt the same she didn't know, and she didn't dare enquire. Occasionally in odd moments she found his eyes on her, watching with concern and doubt. She ignored the hint of caring in his gaze. She had to, she thought savagely. If she let herself believe that Blair Kinnane truly cared for her, then she would go mad.

There was an apartment available for her at the rear of the hospital, but Cari elected to continue living at the Bromptons. She was settled there, she told herself.

There was another, stronger reason. She didn't want to sleep within a hundred metres of Blair. There had to be times when she could get right away from him and from the hospital he worked in. The additional travelling was wearing, but at night when she settled gratefully into her bed at the Bromptons', with Rusty nestled companionably at her side, she didn't regret her decision.

She was so physically tired that here she could sleep. At the hospital, with Blair Kinnane close, she doubted that even physical tiredness would allow her to do so.

Rod rang after a few days, and asked to speak to her. His voice sounded as if he was in a callbox a hundred metres down the street, and Cari had difficulty in believing that he was in America. His voice had regained its lightness, and she was delighted to hear that his father was now considered off the critical list.

'I'll stay on for the month, though, if that's all right, Cari.' Rod sounded guilty.

'Of course it's all right,' Cari said firmly. 'You'd be mad to do anything else. Blair and I are managing just fine.' She grimaced as she spoke. A stretcher was just being wheeled into Casualty and a sister was signalling that she was needed urgently.

'I have to go,' she said to Rod. 'Take care of yourself and your father.'

'I will. And, Cari?'

'Yes?'

'Thank you.'

Cari smiled and put the phone down. It was so good to feel useful again, she thought briefly, before turning her attention to the young man lying on the stretcher waiting for her to see him.

He was suffering from shock and blood loss, she could tell at a glance, and a cursory inspection told her why. His thumb had been torn, almost wrenched from his hand.

What were the alternatives? As Cari set up a drip and administered pain relief she considered the young man's dilemma.

'What happened?' she asked the white-faced youth who had accompanied his friend into the hospital. He was having trouble tearing his gaze from his friend's mangled hand.

'He was trying to ride a horse that was only partly broken,' the boy said faintly. 'The horse took off, and Larry's hand must have got caught in the bridle or something. All I know is that he couldn't get loose. He was screaming, and I couldn't stop the horse. It took me ages.'

Cari glanced sympathetically at his shocked face. 'Thank you for bringing him in,' she said gently. 'We'll look after him now.' She motioned to one of the nurses. 'Sister will take you out to the waiting-room and find you a cup of tea.'

'His thumb. . . Will he lose it?'

Cari looked down at the semi-conscious boy on the stretcher. 'We'll do the best we can,' she said gently. 'It's too early to tell.'

It wasn't. As the morphine took effect and she was able to have a proper look she knew without doubt that the thumb would be lost. Five minutes later, in answer to Cari's urgent summons, Blair strode into Casualty and confirmed it.

'There's nothing there to save,' he said bluntly. 'The thumb's been destroyed. We'll send him down to Perth, though.'

'Why?' queried Cari, surprised. 'If we can't save the thumb then we can repair what's left of the hand as well as surgeons down at Perth.'

Blair shook his head. 'There's another alternative,' he told her. 'It's something that's being done more and more. I'm surprised you haven't seen it.'

'Which is?'

'A thumb substitute. In other words, a big toe.' Blair smiled at her look of amazement. 'I've seen it done, and it works amazingly well,' he continued. 'They take the toe off, perform a bit of cosmetic surgery to make it look like the real thing and stitch it on instead of a thumb. It works almost as well as the real thing, and unless you stare at it closely, it even looks like the real thing.'

'So he has two wounds instead of one.'

Blair nodded, 'They won't do the toe removal now, though. They'll wait until Larry's up to making a decision about it. By sending him to Perth, we're giving the plastic surgeons the chance of removing what's left of the thumb in the best way for later attachment of the toe, if that's what Larry decides to do.'

Cari shook her head in amazement. 'I suppose. . .' she said doubtfully.

'People can do just fine without a big toe,' Blair said firmly. 'They can't do so well without a thumb— especially a right thumb, which this is. I'll check that he's right-handed, but you'll probably find that he'll elect to go ahead with the swap anyway. Loss of a thumb means real disability.'

Their conversation was abruptly cut off as another patient was brought into Casualty. This time it was only a sprain, but it was severe, and it took time to confirm that there wasn't a break. It was the start of a busy afternoon and an even busier evening. For some reason Casualty was becoming more and more popular.

'It's the approach of Slatey Creek Race Week,' Blair explained.

Cari raised her eyes questioningly.

'It sounds like something I should hear about.'

He smiled wearily. 'It's the event of the year on the Slatey Creek calendar. The district comes to a stand-still. Except us. We work twice as hard as at any other time in the year.' He motioned over to the bed where Larry was lying waiting for transport to arrive to take him to Perth. 'Larry's been trying himself out on every wild or half-wild horse he can get his hands on. There's a rodeo at the end of the week, with substantial prize money.'

Cari groaned. 'Then we're likely to see more cuts and sprains and bruises?'

'Larry's only the tip of the iceberg,' said Blair.

When they finally finished in Casualty it was late. Cari still had patients in the hospital to drop in on before she left for the farm.

'Come and have dinner,' said Blair.

She shook her head. 'Maggie will have dinner for me when I get back to the farm.'

He glanced at his watch. 'It's six-thirty now. If you're anything like me you've got another hour's work to go and then a slow drive back to the Bromptons'. Why the hell aren't you living in here?'

'Rusty would miss me,' Cari said lightly, and started to turn away.

Blair gripped her arm and pulled her back to face

him. 'You're afraid of me,' he said softly. 'You're afraid of what's between us. Aren't you, Dr Eliss?'

'I don't know what you're talking about,' Cari said angrily.

'Then prove it.'

'What do you mean?'

He smiled, a dangerously calculating glimmer in the back of his eyes.

'At the end of Race Week Slatey Creek has a Ball. Come with me, Cari Eliss.'

'If Race Week's anything like you say it is then we'll be too busy for any Ball,' she retorted.

'True,' he agreed gravely. 'There's always the chance that we could make it, though.'

'Well, I don't want to go.' She sounded like a defiant child and she knew it.

His grip tightened and he smiled. 'Scared, Dr Eliss?'

'I'm not scared of you.'

'Then that's settled.' He turned away as if he had just finished with a difficult patient. 'I'll pick you up from the Bromptons' at eight.'

Cari was left staring speechlessly after him.

'The Slatey Creek Ball!' Cari was sitting in the Bromptons' living-room, her aching legs resting on cushions on the settee. 'I must be mad. What on earth possessed me?' she wailed.

Maggie grinned. 'I can guess what possessed you,' she ventured. 'If Blair Kinnane crooked his finger at me I'd be forgetting any trifle like a broken pelvis too.'

'Here, watch it!' Jock's startled voice came from behind his three-day-old newspaper and both girls broke into laughter.

'What are you going to wear?' Maggie demanded as the laughter died, and Cari shrugged.

'The white dress, I suppose.'

'He's already seen that.'

'It doesn't matter.'

'Yes, it does.' Maggie swung off her chair and went over to a chest at the edge of the room. 'I'm darned if I'm going to sit back and watch you destroy a good night with apathy. Now just hush your mouth and do what Maggie tells you.'

'It'll be less trouble in the end if you do,' Jock said drily from behind his paper. 'It always is.'

Maggie aimed a slipper at his head. It missed by a metre and he kept reading, unperturbed.

'Well, you're not wearing the white dress,' Maggie said firmly. 'I won't allow it.'

'No, Mother,' Cari said meekly, and Maggie smiled her approval. She was foraging in the depths of the box and finally emerged to stand triumphant.

'How about this?'

It was soft green satin, cut low across the neck, with tiny net sleeves. It curved into the waist and then flared in layer upon layer of tulle and chiffon. Even after years of lying crushed in its storage place, the dress had a life of its own. It shimmered and swayed enticingly, making Cari's eyes light up with pleasure.

Jock was surprised enough to lower his newspaper. 'I remember that,' he said approvingly. Maggie looked up and met his eyes affectionately.

'You should. You proposed when I wore it.'

'Anyone would have,' Jock said simply. He eyed the dress morosely. 'It's got a lot to answer for, that dress.' Maggie picked up her other slipper. As she laughingly threatened him with it he held up a hand in surrender, retired again behind his paper and was silent.

'I couldn't,' Cari said firmly. 'It's your beautiful dress.'

'And a fat lot of good it's doing where it is,' Maggie retorted.

'Then why are you keeping it?'

Maggie looked down fondly at the soft folds spread around her ample form. 'I keep hoping I'll be a size ten again one day,' she smiled. She wrinkled her nose. 'To be honest, I guess I hoped that I'd have a daughter one day who I could shed tears over in it. I don't see Jamie or David fitting the bill, though.' She held it out to Cari. 'It's up to you to save it from a moth-ridden fate.' She glanced at the clock on the wall. 'It's too late to try it tonight. We'll have a fitting tomorrow after dinner.'

It fitted like a glove. Cari looked at her reflection in Maggie's bedroom mirror and couldn't believe her eyes. The shimmering green lifted her complexion, deepening her eyes and accentuating the faint blush of colour in her cheeks. Maggie brushed her hair until it shone like white gold, then pulled it up to a central point, caught it and let it fall in a hundred fair tendrils around her face. The style was simple but wonderful.

Cari gazed at herself for several moments before she could speak. What was she doing? She didn't even want to go to the Ball. Blair Kinnane was the last person in the world she wanted to impress, and here she was, dressed like this.

As she stared at herself in bewilderment the phone rang, and Maggie went to answer it. In a moment she was back.

'It's your frog, Cinderella,' she smiled. 'He's got a mid in who looks like needing a Caesarian. He requires your attendance immediately, if not sooner.'

'You've got your fairy-tales mixed,' Cari laughed. She pulled the dress off, after one more doubtful glance. Cinderella was just how she felt, only with more than Cinders' two roles. Homeless traveller, unemployed and disgraced doctor, overworked doctor for the Flying Doctor Service, and this. . .

She fingered the soft green folds of the dress in confusion, then, taking a deep breath, she reverted to her third role. Dr Eliss was required.

The girl needing a Caesarian was Aboriginal. The plane had just brought her in. She had been labouring with no medical assistance for thirty-six hours and was deeply distressed. Once again Cari could lose herself in her work. It took the combined skill of both her and Blair to end up with a live baby and a recovering mother. And a lot of luck, Cari admitted to herself honestly. The baby was obviously a survivor. She looked down into the prepared humidicrib where the babe was being gently warmed. He had come a tough road.

The mother was stirring as she recovered from the anaesthetic, and Blair motioned Cari away. He ushered her out of the door. Two older women, both Aboriginal, were waiting in the corridor. Blair spoke briefly to them and watched as they went in to the girl. Then he took Cari by the arm and guided her away.

'Let them be for a while,' he said to Cari. 'The girl's had a dreadful time, and if she wakes up to nothing familiar she's just as likely to go into shock. This is a far cry from what she's used to. She belongs to one of the nomadic tribes that hardly come near a settlement for months on end.'

'But what's she been doing for ante-natal care?'

'Nothing.'

'Nothing?'

Blair shook his head. 'If I'd known about her I would

have made a point of catching up with her group. But I didn't. She's been extremely lucky that they were a reasonable distance from a homestead and the women could get help for her.'

'The women?'

Blair nodded. 'It's women's business, this bearing babies,' he said. 'We're going to have to keep her in hospital a while, but from here on she's your patient, Dr Eliss. She's going to have enough to cope with, without a man examining her.'

'Such as?'

'Well, the diet, for one thing. I'll be willing to bet she's never eaten mutton or chicken, maybe not even beef, in her life. Her people are hardly in a position to cultivate vegetables. If we served her up lamb chops and three vegetables followed by apple pie and ice cream then in all probability we'd make her sick. Still, to a certain exent she'll have to adjust to some of our food.'

'Do you cook bush food here?' Cari asked, startled.

'A bit—we have to. The Aboriginal community represents a quarter of our patients. We get in a regular supply of things such as emu meat.'

'Ugh!'

Blair laughed. 'That's probably what the girl in there will say when she sees a lamb chop.'

A sister was approaching from down the corridor, and Cari looked up to recognise Liz.

'Mrs Findlay in room three is complaining of pain, Blair,' she smiled.

Blair nodded. 'I'll see you tomorrow, then, Dr Eliss,' he said formally and strode briskly away. Cari was left standing with Liz. She started to move, but Liz put her hand on her arm to detain her.

'I hear you're going to the Ball with our Dr Kinnane,' she said pleasantly.

Cari looked at the girl curiously. 'Yes.' There was nothing else she could think of to add.

Liz swung her hair back triumphantly from her face. 'I wish you joy of him,' she said sweetly. 'And I can tell you now that he's not worth the effort. You'll get exactly nowhere. I've decided to cut my losses completely in that direction,' she confided. 'I'm going to the Ball with Ray Blainey—he's the son of the biggest landowner in the district.'

She ended on a note of exultance, cast Cari a pitying look and swept away. Cari was left looking after her with disdain.

She drove home slowly. It seemed then the truth that Blair had not become involved past a superficial level since his wife died. Blair's words came back to her. He had said he had not slept with another woman since he left his wife.

So where did that leave him now? He had taken her to him, committing himself in an act of love to a woman who was now rejecting him utterly. Didn't that leave him as exposed as she was?

She shook herself angrily. Blair Kinnane would have to look out for himself. If she worried about his emotional state she would go mad. She couldn't even work out her own.

Blair was right when he said that they would be busy in Race Week. The week before was bad enough as the youth of the district went into training, but as the start of the week approached, Slatey Creek was filled to bursting. Every house had guests, the pub was spilling over at the seams and a mass of tents appeared down by the river bed.

The sprains, cuts and bruises Cari and Blair had been treating were augmented by the mass of minor ailments that the visitors had been saving for their trip to town. Morning surgeries had three times their normal numbers of people.

They never seemed to be easy problems either. They were things which couldn't be discussed easily over the air, things which had been 'saved up' for the trip to Slatey Creek, such as suspected arthritis, or bad backs, or even such less tangible problems such as women wanting to talk about a husband who was drinking too much. None of these could be dealt with in ten minutes. Cari found herself willing Rod to return. He was not due back until two days after the ball to celebrate the end of Race Week.

If only the tension between her and Blair didn't exist. If only she hadn't allowed him to make love to her. . .

As well as the tiredness she was feeling because of the work-load she was imposing on her still healing body, there was also fatigue caused by the tension he engendered in her. Every time she was near him, she could feel it. In medical emergencies it submerged, but never quite disappeared. As soon as her mind was no longer wholly occupied with medicine, she was desperately aware of him.

And he of her. No matter how formally he treated her, Cari knew that Blair was still aware of her as a woman. She could see it in his eyes, resting on her in rare moments of calm. She could feel it in the almost palpable tension between them.

'I've only to get through another week,' she told herself firmly. Already she was packing her truck, starting to reload her equipment that she had salvaged from the wreck of her last truck. When Rod returned she wanted to leave, immediately.

It was as much as she could do to find half an hour of daylight to do any packing at all.

The excitement in the town was contagious. It was such a tiny community that it was impossible to stay locked within the confines of the hospital and not be caught up in the activities. As well as the extra workload caused by the sheer number of people in the town, it was also necessary that a doctor be in attendance at each of the race or rodeo meetings. Cari had been stunned when she heard that, but after viewing the casualties caused by the first rodeo she had to agree on the sense of the ruling.

Normally it was Blair who made his way across the dusty paddocks in the ambulance van to wait for the next batch of casualties, but occasionally Cari took a turn. She was horrified.

'Just wrap it up, will you Doc? I'm into the second round.'

Cari stared down at the fractured finger and up to the impatient youth holding it out to her. She shook her head.

'You want to go back out into that?' She gestured out to the mill of noise, heat, horses, dust and people.

'Doc, come on!' The youth nearly shook his finger with impatience. 'I've only got ten minutes to be back in the saddle!'

'They're mad,' she told Blair firmly when she returned to the hospital at the end of the day's events. He smiled.

'Not mad,' he contradicted her. 'This is the highlight of their year. Most of these kids have a really quiet time for fifty-one weeks of the year. They've got to let them let their hair down now.'

'But they're trying to kill themselves!' she protested.

'Not as much as city kids doing thirty kilometres an hour over the speed-limit on freeways,' Blair said firmly.

He looked at her appraisingly, and once again Cari felt the surge of awareness that his gaze on her caused.

'Anyway, Dr Eliss, you're a fine one to talk about taking risks.'

'I didn't take risks.'

'No?'

Cari's colour mounted. 'If you'll excuse me, Dr Kinnane.' She glanced at her watch. 'It's nine o'clock. If I leave now I might just have eight hours' sleep tonight.'

They were approaching the front entrance of the hospital as they were speaking.

'If you stayed in here you could have nine,' said Blair.

Cari glared up at him. 'Or less, if you had anything to do with it,' she snapped.

He nodded gravely. 'There is that,' he agreed. He laid a hand on her shoulder and turned her back to him. 'Cari, I don't understand what's going on,' he said.

Cari jerked away from his touch. 'I don't know what you mean,' she said quietly.

'Cari, for all you're trying to pretend it didn't happen, we made love. We weren't drunk. We were perfectly, absolutely sober, and we wanted each other very much.' He put his hand back to hold her possessively. 'I didn't want this either,' he told her. 'I don't understand what it is between us, but I can feel it. All I have to do is look at you and I feel it like a tight wire drawing us together.'

'So you think we should just keep sleeping together

until we get it out of our system,' Cari said, in a hard small voice.

'Something like that,' he admited. 'Cari, I want you. God knows why, but I want you.'

'Despite my being a negligent, spoiled child, you want me.' Cari gave a short, bitter laugh.

'You don't give me a chance,' he said quietly.

'I don't see any reason for giving anyone a chance,' she said savagely. 'You don't do it in this game. I've left myself exposed before and all it's done is cause me heartache.' She swung the heavy front door open and Blair shifted his grip to hold it for her. 'Goodnight, Dr Kinnane,' she said dismissively.

Blair stood on the top step, watching her retreat across the car park.

'Goodnight, Dr Eliss. Don't take any of those risks between here and the Bromptons'.'

'I won't,' she said curtly.

'Cari?'

'Yes?' Cari had reached her truck. She opened the driver's door and stood looking back at the figure waching her from the step.

'Don't forget now,' he chided her gently. 'I'm picking you up at eight tomorrow night.'

'I'll bring myself in.'

'A promise is a promise,' Blair said blandly. 'You agreed to come to the Ball with me. I intend to do it in style. Eight at the Bromptons'.'

'But that's crazy!' Cari expostulated.

'Goodnight, Dr Eliss.'

CHAPTER TWELVE

FOR a while it looked as if Cari's prayers were going to be answered and she was not going to be able to go the Ball. The last day of Race Week was as busy as any that had gone previously. Towards evening, though, on the night of the Ball, the steady trickle of casualties dried up and Cari was left free.

As many staff as possible had been rostered on during the last few days. Much to the relief of the two doctors, Maggie had declared her holiday over, and was now back working full-time. Having finished her day's work now, she had come to find Cari.

'Dr Eliss, if that's all, I think it's time we got ourselves home and decked out in our finery,' she announced.

'Are you and Jock coming too?' Cari asked with pleasure.

'We've never missed,' Maggie said firmly. She linked her arm through Cari's and gave her an impatient tug. 'Let's go, Dr Eliss. You may look beautiful by slipping on a dress and batting your eyelids, but for me it requires a little more application!'

Cari smiled and allowed herself to be led. Now Maggie was back at work, they were sharing transport whenever possible.

Once back at the farm she dressed slowly and with care. It was the first time she had made a real effort for well over a year. As she put the final touches to her make-up she made faces at herself in the mirror. It was as if there were two personalities warring within her.

One of them didn't want to be anywhere near the Slatey Creek Ball. The other. . .

A tiny part of her was whispering that this would be the last time she would spend with Blair Kinnane. After this Blair would return to being an outback doctor who lived on a different continent from Cari Eliss, ex-doctor.

Cari grimaced and turned her attention back to her face. What was she doing?

The sound of the dogs heralding a vehicle's approach made her start. She put down the blusher she was holding and stepped back to look in the mirror as Maggie came into the room.

'Wow!' Maggie said simply.

Cari looked critically at her reflection. The dress was lovely. Whenever she moved it shimmered and glistened with a thousand soft green reflections of light. It cupped her breasts, accentuating their soft swell, curved in to show her tiny waist to perfection and then fanned out to sway alluringly around her hips.

Maggie had done her hair. The same simple style she had tried the night Cari had first put on the dress needed little adjusting. It shone in tiny golden tendrils around her face.

'Come and see, Jock!' Maggie called to her husband. She herself was dressed simply but stunningly in a very low-cut black dress which showed her more ample figure off to perfection. Jock came in, looked at Cari, laughed and reached to hug his wife.

'Second-best woman I've ever seen, I reckon,' he said appreciatively.

'Get on with you,' laughed Maggie. She stood back and looked affectionately at her husband. 'You don't scrub up too badly yourself.'

The dogs' barking rose to a frenzy and a vehicle pulled up below the houe.

'Do we need anyone else in this mutual admiration society?' demanded Jock. 'Let's just lock the door and look at each other for a while. What happens if the great Dr Kinnane doesn't like green, Cari?'

'Then he hasn't got eyes in his head,' Maggie retorted. She gave her husband a push. 'Go and let him in, Jock.'

There was no need to worry. Whatever Blair Kinnane's previous sentiments on the colour green might have been, it was immediately obvious that on Cari he approved of it very much. He was laughing at a comment of Jock's as Cari emerged from the bedroom. As he saw her he fell silent, the smile fading from his face.

Cari felt her colour mounting. This evening was to be a farewell by her to Slatey Creek, to this man. She mustn't allow him to unsettle her.

In his immaculately tailored dinner-suit, he looked almost stunningly good-looking. The sun-bleached tips of his deep brown hair accentuated the tan of his face. His wide mouth and gentle smile made her heart lurch within her.

She mustn't. . . Her eyes met his and the colour rose further.

'Can I offer anyone a drink?' Jock was enjoying himself, trying not very successfully to hide his amusement. Maggie glared at him and he grinned unrepentantly.

'Thank you, but we won't, Jock,' Blair said firmly. 'I've got other plans for Cari.'

Maggie raised her eyebrows and Jock laughed. 'Say no more,' he said expansively, pulling the door wide and ushering them out. 'Maggie and I were young once ourselves.'

'Excuse me!' said his other half.

Blair smiled. 'I sense a domestic,' he said to Cari. 'Shall we leave?'

It seemed she had no choice. He held out his hand. Hesitatingly she took it and was propelled gently to the passenger side of his vehicle. They left Maggie and Jock on the veranda steps, smiling after them.

'So what are these plans?' Cari asked as they swung out of the road gate.

He looked down at her, a dangerous glint in his eye. 'I had thought of having drinks with the Bromptons,' he conceded. 'Until I saw you.'

For a moment Cari was silent, lost as to what to say. Finally she found her voice. 'So now what?'

He glanced back down at her and laughed. 'There's no need to sound so scared, Dr Eliss. I don't intend to rape you.'

'Well, that's a comfort,' she said with asperity.

'I imagine it is,' he agreed. He slowed suddenly and pulled off the main road into town, taking a track that led to what seemed to be a long, low ridge of rocks in the distance.

'The deal was that you take me to the Ball,' Cari said angrily.

'So it was,' he agreed. 'So it is.'

'Well?'

The truck was starting to climb a gradual incline.

'I don't know how it is where you come from,' Blair said, 'but here eight o'clock is only the official starting time for a ball. For heaven's sake. . .' he gestured around them, 'it's not even dark yet. The caterers and the band arrive at eight o'clock.' He looked across at her again and his gaze raked her appreciatively. 'Certainly not the belle of the Ball.'

'So we're filling in time?' Cari chose to ignore the last remark.

'You could call it that,' Blair agreed. 'Or perhaps it's just that I know the chances of being back on duty by the end of the evening are somewhere around ninety per cent.'

'And what has that got to do with it?' Cari sounded like a shrew, but she was unsettled and anxious.

'Dr Eliss.'

'Yes?'

He reached a finger over and placed it gently over her lips. 'Shut up.'

Ten minutes later they reached the top of the ridge. Blair pulled the vehicle off the track and parked beside a large clump of smooth rocks. He climbed out and came around to help Cari from her seat.

'So now what?'

He smiled, refusing to be discouraged by her surliness. 'Now we climb, Dr Eliss.'

'Up there?' Cari looked up in disbelief to the outcrop of rock. In flat shoes, with pelvic bones that weren't still recovering, she might have managed it. Now, there was no way. 'I can't,' she said flatly.

He nodded. 'Perhaps I should have re-phrased that,' he said pleasantly. He reached to grip her firmly, and with one smooth motion swung her up and into his arms. 'I climb,' he corrected himself, smiling down into her indignant face. 'You lie back and enjoy the ride.' He turned to the rock face and started climbing steadily.

'You're mad!' Cari started to struggle, but his grip was like iron.

'You know,' he said pleasantly, 'these rocks are really very hard, Cari. It wouldn't do your pelvis any good at all to be dropped hard down on to them. If I were you I'd keep still, there's a good girl.'

Cari could do nothing else. She subsided, glaring at him.

He really was so good-looking it was unfair, she thought savagely, looking up at him. The look of him in his dark suit, his deep grey eyes concentrating on his footing on the rough ground, his hair tousled by the faint wind. . . It wasn't fair. He made her heart knot into an irretrievable tangle just by being there. Just by being. . .

She lay back passively in his arms, the soft green folds of her dress falling around her. She felt foolish and very young.

Finally they reached the top. Blair set her down carefully on the smooth surface of the highest rock, then sat down beside her. He gripped her shoulders and pointed her down, the way they had come.

'This is what we're here for,' he said simply. 'Watch.'

Below them the flat, barren ground stretched away to a distant horizon. Away in the distance the tiny settlement of Slatey Creek was hardly larger than the ridge they were occupying. It certainly didn't make any impression on the vastness of the landscape around it. The earth was dusky red, dry and arid, with blackboys and occasional tufts of some hardy bushes dotted across the earth. As the sky met the land, the sun was a great flame of orange, sinking fast towards the horizon.

The colours in the sky were indescribable—orange, apricot, pink and vivid red. It looked as if a massive ball of flame was scorching the horizon. Cari caught her breath in wonder. At her side, Blair was silent as he watched.

For perhaps fifteen minutes they stayed speechless, watching as the sun played out its parting moments of glory. Cari had never seen such a sunset. As the fiery ball disappeared from view the colours slowly softened and faded. Finally the sky was left the soft grey-blue of approaching night, with only a faint streak of tinged light at the horizon to tell the story of what had just taken place.

'Well,' Blair said at last, 'what do you think of our evening's entertainment?'

Cari was still almost too awed to talk. It was as if, by breaking the silence, she would break the spell around them and admit the mundanity of the outside world.

'It was wonderful,' she whispered.

Blair nodded, his eyes leaving the horizon and falling on the girl seated at his side. 'I come up here often,' he told her, 'when things get too much for me, below. When I lose a patient, or when I'm just so damned overworked I can't get my perspective right any more I come up here. It helps,' he said simply.

Cari nodded. Why did she feel like crying? This man, with his looks, his voice, his perception. . . To be loved by a man such as this. . .

'Cari?'

'Yes?' She looked up at him wonderingly.

For a long drawn-out moment they stayed, searching each other's eyes. Then, very slowly, Blair's mouth lowered to meet Cari's lips.

It was the first kiss of lovers, the soft exploration of an awakening awareness. There was no rush, no fierce passion, just a gentle, tentative questioning. They sat, two tiny figures dwarfed by the endless landscape of barren plains around them, not touching except with their lips, endlessly joined.

Cari couldn't guess how long it lasted. Its sweetness

sent a poignant joy spreading through her. It was as if
a thousand nightingales were singing within her head,
building to an unbearable crescendo of beauty. This
man. . . He was all she wanted, all she would ever
want.

Finally they drew apart. Their eyes mirrored what
they were feeling, and, with a shock of recognition, she
saw her own joy reflected in Blair's grey eyes. He
reached out and held her gently against him, stroking
the golden hair as her face fell against his chest.

She could feel the rhythm of his heart, beating
strongly. It was as if she was a lost child who had finally
found her home. Here was peace. Here was a sanc-
tuary. Here was love.

The darkness deepened around them, but still they
stayed unmoving, neither wishing to break the magic
surrounding them. The soft warmth of the night air
caressed their skin, enveloping them in its comforting
folds. Cari nestled closer, closer to her love.

Finally Blair stirred. He gripped her shoulders,
dropped a kiss lightly on top of the fair head and held
her away from him.

'Cari?'

'Mmm.' The response came from a long way away.

'What's haunting you?' His voice was infinitely
gentle. 'Can't you tell me?'

The dreamlike quality faded. Cari looked up and
met the concerned grey eyes watching her. She shook
her head mutely.

'Why not?' He bent down and kissed her lightly on
the forehead. 'Cari. . .' His voice was suddenly unsure.
'This thing between us—it's special. It's too special to
throw away because of lack of honesty.' He lifted her
chin and held her face up to him. 'Cari, when I left my
wife she was with her third lover in as many months. I

swore I could never love another woman. And here I am, Cari, trusting you, opening myself to you. Now you're going to have to do the same, Cari. So tell me.'

Cari's mind swelled in panic. This was too precious, too fragile to risk. How could she watch the love in his eyes turn sour? Better to leave. . .

'No.' The word was a whisper hanging between them.

'Why not?'

'Because you won't believe me.' She pulled away from his grasp and stood up.

'Try me.'

She shook her head. She reached out her hands and took Blair's strong ones between hers. She forced calm into her voice. 'You're right, Blair. I know that what's happening between us could be something. . .' She faltered and her voice trailed off. Once again she forced herself to continue.

'I'm only here for two more days,' she said. 'In two days I'll be gone, and I don't want to see disbelief and uncertainty in your eyes before I go.'

'What makes you so sure you'd see it if you told me?'

'Because it's inevitable.' She pulled her hands away from him. 'For nearly eighteen months I've been labelled a negligent, incompetent doctor, and, as well as that, a liar. I can cope with your thinking I'm negligent and incompetent. Don't make me add the last one to your list.'

Blair frowned, his brow furrowed in the dim light. 'What makes you so sure I wouldn't believe you?' he repeated.

'Because nobody does,' she said simply. She put a hand to her face and rubbed her fingers tiredly across her eyes. 'Eighteen months ago I had a family who were proud of me and my achievements, and a fiancé who I thought loved me. They listened to my story and they branded me, just as the judge and the lawyers and everyone else branded me.' She looked helplessly up at Blair. 'Blair, I'm falling in love all over again,' she said in a tiny voice. 'And I couldn't bear it. It's better that I just go.'

'You'd run rather than take the chance?'

She nodded. 'I've been through all I can bear. If it happens again I'll fall to pieces.'

'So for the rest of your life, there's going to be no trust?'

'How can there be?' she asked despairingly.

'And if I ask you to marry me, without knowing the details of your murky past?'

Cari gasped. 'Don't joke with me, Blair,' she pleaded.

'Who's joking?' He gripped her hard. 'It seems to me that you're throwing me the worst of insults. Just because your family haven't stood by you in the past, you're judging everyone, even me. You're not giving me a chance. And for whatever reason, God knows, I've fallen deeply, irrevocably in love with you. I want you. I need you. To hell with what you've done in the past——it's the Cari Eliss that I'm holding now that I want.'

'But. . .' She stopped helplessly.

'But what?' he demanded savagely. 'Cari, is it the fact that I've been married? Can't you accept that our past can be put aside? My ex-wife no longer matters, just as your ex-fiancé doesn't matter. What matters is now, Cari. What we're feeling for each other.'

'And when you learn the truth?'

'Well, if you won't tell me then I'm just going to

have to take a chance on that too,' he said grimly.
'Forget the past. Forget the future and marry me.'

'That's crazy!'

'Is it?' His grip on her shoulders was suddenly
unbearably tight. 'What's crazy is your distrust. I trust
you, Cari. But then I love you. Do you love me enough
to trust me?'

'No!' It was a cry of pain. She broke away from him
and turned away. 'Blair, don't—please!'

'Cari. . .'

'No!' She warded him off with her hands. 'Don't you
see that I can't love any more? Don't you see that? It's
not fair to twist you up in my convoluted existence.
I've had my chances at happiness and I've blown them.
You don't want me. Once I'm out of your sight you'll
be thanking your lucky stars for your escape.' She
looked bleakly down the rocky slope, wishing she could
manage the climb herself.

'Take me home, please, Blair,' she said tiredly. 'I've
had enough.'

For a long moment there was silence. Then Blair
strode forward and picked the slight girl back up in his
arms.

'Let's go to the Ball, then, Cari,' he said gently. 'If
you won't marry me, at least you still can dance with
me.'

The Ball was well under way when they arrived. Cari
was still feeling limp and shocked. All she wanted to
do was to crawl back to the Bromptons' and put her
head under her pillow, never to emerge, but Blair was
having none of it.

'You promised to come to the Ball with me, Dr
Eliss. I'm not aware of any escape clauses in the

contract caused by minor disagreements.' His voice attempted lightness, but it didn't quite come off.

They made a preoccupied couple in the noisy, bois-terous crowd. The population of Slatey Creek was out to enjoy itself, come what may. This was their night of the year.

Blair was a well-known and loved personality, Cari realised as soon as she walked in the door on his arm. He was greeted on all sides with friendliness and welcome.

As was she. The local young men were clearly delighted to see her without the encumbrances of her walking sticks, and she was inundated as soon as she walked in the door by prospective dancing partners.

Blair was having none of it. His grip on her arm was proprietorial. For the night, at least, Cari belonged to him.

They moved from one dance to another, Cari never more than an arm's length away from Blair. In the intervals between dances, he chatted cheerfully to the couples surrounding them, but always he made it obvious to those around him that he and Cari were a couple. He skilfully included her in the conversation, hiding with ease the fact that she was silent and preoccupied.

Towards midnight, Cari's legs stared to ache, a grinding hurt that masked the pain she was feeling in her heart. Blair sensed the slowing of her steps. As the band moved into a slow number his grip tightened and he bent towards her.

'Tired, my love?'

Cari nodded mutely. She was past arguing.

He turned to lead her off the floor and, as he did so, one of the people at the table where he had left the radio signalled him that he was wanted. He grimaced.

'It looks as if our evening might be over anyway,' he said ruefully.

It was. It was the charge sister at the hospital.

'There's been a call from out at Hitchins', Dr Kinnane.' The nurse's voice sounded strange and disembodied on the little receiver. 'Mrs Hitchins says a car came by there five minutes ago at high speed, then they heard an almighty crash. Bob has taken his truck up to investigate now, but his wife thought she'd better warn you that you might be needed.'

'I'll come up to the hospital now.' Blair put down the receiver and turned to Cari. 'It looks as if I might be going out in the plane,' he told her. 'The Hitchins' place is about ninety kilometres from here over some pretty rough country. I'll go back to the hospital and wait for Bob to call through, but Mrs Hitchins is a sensible woman. She wouldn't have called unless she was pretty sure I'd be needed.' He looked at Cari, assessing her tired face. 'What would you like to do? You're too tired to stay.'

It was true. Cari's legs were aching and emotionally she was too drained to continue making cheerful chat with the locals.

'Will you need me?' she asked.

Blair shook his head. 'Not initially,' he said. 'Only one doctor goes with the plane. If it's nasty I might need you later, if we bring casualties in.' He glanced at his watch. 'What I suggest is that I take you back to my rooms.' He put out a hand as if to ward off her protests. 'If I have to go I'll be gone for a couple of hours at least. You can get some sleep and be there if I need you later on.'

'Blair. . .'

'Come on.' He ignored her involuntary protest, took her hand and led her out through the crowded room.

By the time they got back to the hospital, Mrs Hitchins had called in again. The charge sister met them at the door. Her gaze took in the appearance of the two of them, coming to rest on the linked hands. Blair had taken Cari's hand to assist her out of the truck and had not relinquished it. Cari made to pull away, but his hold tightened. It was as if he were determined to make some sort of statement.

'It sounds nasty,' the sister said, her eyes still on the linked hands. 'Mrs Hitchins has gone down to the crash herself now. Her husband came back to get her, plus blankets and tools for trying to free the kids from the car.'

'Kids?'

'Four teenagers. They think two are dead. The car hit a kangaroo, and Mrs Hitchins reckons they would have been travelling around two hundred kilometres an hour when they went past their place.'

'Have you contacted Luke?' Luke was the on-call pilot for the night.

'He's down at the hangar already. I rang him before I contacted you.'

Blair nodded. 'Come on, Cari, let's go.'

'Where?' she asked.

He laughed shortly. 'I need to change and you need to go to bed—pronto. It sounds as if we'll be working for the rest of the night.'

Blair's flat opened off the rear of the hospital building. He thrust open the door and strode into the bedroom.

'The bed's in here,' he called unnecessarily. He was stripping off his suit as he spoke, pulling on more serviceable clothes. 'Get into it, block out everything else and sleep. Even if you can't sleep, don't you dare move those legs of yours until I get back,' he ordered.

'Sister can get the theatre set up and ready. If we're going to have to operate then I don't want you falling over halfway through.'

'Have I ever?' she protested, and he smiled.

'I guess not,' he conceded, 'and your legs have been a darn sight more fragile than this. I'm not taking any chances, however.' He pointed firmly to the pillows. 'Bed, Dr Eliss.'

'Yes, sir,' she said meekly.

Blair could order her to bed, but he couldn't order her to sleep. She lay watching the moonlight's wavering patterns on the roof of the little bedroom. This bed was strange and yet familiar. It smelt like him, felt like him. . . It was as if his presence was enveloping her, protecting and cherishing even now.

The events of the evening swirled and moved through her tired mind. Blair Kinnane had asked her to marry him. She shook her head against the pillow, still caught in shock.

To marry Blair. . . There was nothing on this earth she would rather do. He was her man. She knew it now, as surely as she could ever know anything. Her engagement to Harvey had been a stupid interlude, a mistake which she should be grateful that events had released her from.

She loved Blair; she acknowledged it to herself with surety. She also knew that she couldn't drag him down.

She remembered the words her father had said, on that final, hurtful visit home.

'Your disgrace doesn't just drag you down. It drags down everybody you associate with. If you can't be a competent doctor then don't go near medicine, and stay away, right away, from us. I'll be damned if I'll see mud being slung against innocent family members because of your lies and incompetence.'

They were all there, her father and her brothers, all with hard, implacable faces, with her mother weeping quietly in the background.

They were all people who she thought loved her. But the first touch of stigma and she had been cast adrift.

She couldn't bear it. To let Blair go on thinking she was incompetent was bad enough, but to try and explain and have him turn against her with the same eyes would be ten times worse. She put her face in the pillow and wept.

She must have gone to sleep. The next thing she was aware of was the light being switched on full. The charge sister was standing over her.

'You're needed, I'm afraid,' she said sympathetically. Like most of the staff she still had trouble with the transition of Cari from patient to doctor. She held out the change of clothes that Cari always kept in the staff-room in case she had to make a change during the day. There was never any guarantee, with medicine, that clothes could be kept clean for a full working day. 'I thought you might need these.'

Cari sat up, and winced at the harshness of the light. She took the proffered dress gratefully. She didn't fancy putting the green evening dress back on. The clock on the bedside table said half-past three.

'What's happening?' she asked abruptly. The sister was already starting to walk back out of the door. She hesitated only momentarily.

'There were four boys in the car,' she told Cari. 'Two were killed instantly. One died while they were trying to get him out of the car and one's back here. He's got massive internal haemorrhaging. Dr Kinnane's already in Theatre.' She shook her head.

'Not that he's got much hope of saving him,' she added as she disappeared.

Cari didn't think so either. One look at the boy and she realised the odds they were facing. She glanced up at Blair's set face, and wondered what they must have had to do to get him out alive. By the look of it, to keep him alive even this long had been a gigantic struggle.

They had to try.

The damage was immense. There was a massive head injury. It was far too early to guess the possible outcome of that. There were broken bones, and a ruptured bowel, bladder and spleen. Everywhere they looked there was more damage. All they could do was to try and curtail the bleeding, and hope.

It wasn't enough. Whatever they were doing was not sufficient to hold the boy's fragile grip on life. Thirty minutes after Cari had been woken, the boy quietly slipped away from them.

There was a long silence in the theatre. Cari looked up at Blair's exhausted face and her heart went out to him. He looked grey and defeated.

'Come back to the flat and I'll make you some coffee,' she said quietly.

He nodded. They cleaned up silently.

By the time they had finished in the theatre, the first of the distraught parents had arrived. Cari left Blair to it. It was Blair, the doctor they knew, whom they needed to speak to. She went back to the little apartment at the rear of the hospital, put on the coffee and waited.

An hour later he came in. The greyness of his face had deepened. She looked up from where she was sitting at the table, and suddenly she could bear it no longer. She went to him, put her arms round him and held him to her.

For a long while they didn't speak. Behind them the coffee hissed and bubbled gently on the stove. Blair was holding her as if the warmth of her body was somehow breathing into him a strength that he had lost. Finally he released her, sank into a chair and buried his face in his hands. Cari turned to the stove to pour coffee. She handed him a mug and watched sympathetically as he drank it.

'OK?' she asked as he put the empty mug down. He shook his head.

'No, not OK.' He ran his hand wearily through his hair. 'It'll be a long time before I get over that one.' He sat up and stretched. 'Kids and alcohol,' he sighed. 'Every one of those kids was dead drunk. The car was littered with empty bottles.' He stared reflectively into the dregs of his coffee-cup.

'I know them all,' he continued. 'They're all four damned fine kids, boys who'd make terrific farmers in the future, great husbands, good citizens. And it's all wasted because they got drunk and thought they could drive better than anyone else on the road.' He looked up at Cari. 'And I'm supposed to miraculously save their lives,' he said bitterly. 'I didn't have a chance. They didn't give themselves one.'

Cari took the coffee-cup from him, washed it and dried it meticulously. Blair didn't move. She put down the towel.

'I'd better go,' she said quietly.

He looked up. 'How are you going to get back to the farm?' he asked.

'I'll borrow the hospital car,' she said. 'Maggie'll bring it in first thing in the morning.'

Blair rose, pushing the chair roughly over the vinyl floor. 'Cari?'

'Yes?'

He reached out and pulled her against him. 'Please stay.'

She folded into him, fitting against his body as if he had been moulded to fit her shape. She had no defence against this man.

'For tonight,' she whispered softly. 'It changes nothing, but for tonight. If it's what you want.'

He didn't answer. For the third time that night she was picked up and carried, this time to where the already rumpled sheets of the big double bed lay waiting for them.

Cari woke as dawn filtered through the wide, screened window. A soft breeze was stirring, rustling the blinds. Her back was curved into Blair's body, and he held her possessively, even in sleep.

This was how she would have to remember him, she thought bleakly. This was how love could be, forever and ever, if she had not twisted her life into its stupid, bitter fate. To lie here like this, every morning of her life. . .

Only one, she reminded herself. Tomorrow Rod would return and she could be gone.

'Would be gone.' She said the words firmly aloud, and Blair stirred uneasily in his sleep. His grip tightened. Cari glanced at the clock. Six a.m. Perhaps there could be two more hours before she would have to stir, before the pressures of their day started again. She was under no illusion as to what the day held. With four unexpected deaths the formalities alone would take most of the day.

Two hours. She lay in her protected curve, savouring

his warmth. Just to lie here perfectly still for two hours was all that she could ask. Then Blair's arms tightened even further and she knew that he too was awake. His hand moved tentatively down the silken smoothness of her bare skin, feeling the contours of her body.

She turned in the bed to face him, and met his eyes. They were hazy with sleep, but as she watched with love they deepened until there was no mistaking the desire written there. His hands gently stroked, long sweeping movements that followed the lines of her body, from her shoulders, down to cup the gentle swell of her breasts, around to run down the small of her back and then down the long line of her thighs.

Her thighs stirred of their own accord and she moved her body in to press against the beloved skin, to feel with her body the urgency of his need. Joyfully she realised that her two hours of stillness weren't to be.

Somehow they managed to tear themselves apart, to take again the steps to ensure that in nine months their act of love would not result in a baby. Then they were free, to take each other with the fierce hunger of their need. Their bodies merged once again into a triumphant single being.

Afterwards, Blair slept again. Cari could not. She was sated with love, her body as fulfilled as it was ever likely to be again. She lay watching Blair's sleeping face, trying to memorise every inch of him.

Finally she heard the noises of the hospital stirring. She looked again at the clock. Any minute now Blair would be needed.

There would be times today when she would have to see him, as they both worked to get through the tasks already mounting. This, though, would have to be her proper goodbye.

She leaned forward and kissed him lightly on the lips. He didn't stir. 'Goodbye, Blair,' she said softly. 'Goodbye, my love.'

She slipped soundlessly out of the bed, pulled on her clothes and left him sleeping.

CHAPTER THIRTEEN

Two hours later, showered, breakfasted and changed, Cari was ready for work again. There were no questions from Maggie or Jock as to her whereabouts the night before. By the time Cari had arrived home the whole district had heard of the tragedy. Cari was met with hot coffee and sympathy.

'Your dress is still back at the hospital,' she apologised to Maggie.

'I wasn't planning on wearing it this morning.' Maggie brushed her apology aside with a reassuring smile. 'It's just as well you had another outfit at the hospital. It wasn't what you'd want to wear when talking to distressed relatives.'

'Blair did that,' Cari said briefly, and Maggie nodded.

'You and Blair?' she probed tentatively. 'Did you enjoy the Ball?'

'Blair did, I think.'

Maggie poured her another cup of coffee. 'But not you?'

'I was tired,' Cari said defensively. 'And my legs hurt.' Even to herself the words sounded trite and petty.

'So you're still planning to leave us?' Maggie persisted.

'Why wouldn't I be?' Cari demanded. 'As soon as Rod returns I'll be leaving.' She looked up and caught the hurt in Maggie's eyes. Impulsively she stood and gave the older woman a hug. 'Oh, Maggie, that sounded dreadful! It's not as if I'm not fond of you. It's just that I have to go.'

'We hoped that your fondness for Blair might make you stay,' Maggie said gently.

Cari looked at her for a long moment. This lady saw too much.

'It's my fondness for Blair that's making it so urgent that I should go,' she said eventually.

Maggie's eyes met hers. There was a drawn-out silence before she finally nodded. She asked no further questions.

Fifteen minutes later Cari pulled into the hospital car park. Parked in front of the entrance was Rod's car.

Rod wasn't due back until tomorrow. Cari stared at the little car. It was unmistakable, a white sports car, totally out of place in this rough country. One of the nurses going to Perth on leave had driven it down to wait for him. She let out her breath in a huge sigh of relief. Now she could go. She could walk into the building, hand over her work to Rod and leave.

The hospital waiting-room was crowded, and Cari recognised a couple of faces from the night before. There was a mill of distressed relatives, and she could guess why. The bodies would be being brought in this morning and identification would have to take place. She grimaced. Blair was there, already surrounded, and Cari's heart went out to him. He was going to have a dreadful day.

She made her way through to Rod's office, the office that she had been using. As she suspected, Rod was in there with the door firmly shut. He looked up as she entered and signalled her to shut the door behind her.

'For heaven's sake, shut it, will you, Cari? I've been

back for thirty minutes and I've had three people wanting me already.

'What it is to be popular,' Cari said lightly. She went over and kissed him on the cheek. 'Welcome back, Rod. What are you doing back here early?'

'I didn't mean to be,' he responded, giving her a hard hug in return. 'I got back to Perth two days ago and was going to spend a day in town, but the forecast is for rain and lots of it. I decided, with my car, I'd better get up here before it hit.'

'Rain?' Cari gazed out of the window at the cloudless sky. 'I didn't think it ever rained here.'

'Well, when it does it has to be seen to be believed,' Rod assured her. 'And my car's not really built for coping with mud puddles, much less a torrential downpour.'

Cari looked dubiously out of the window, before turning back. 'I hope you're wrong,' she said. 'I guess my truck is a lot better fitted for hard work than your car, but I'm not all that fussed about driving in heavy rain.' She shrugged off her concern. There was nothing she could do about it. She was going anyway. 'How are things at home?' she asked Rod.

'A darn sight better than they are here, I imagine,' he said grimly. 'This is some reception you've organised for me!'

'It'll settle,' Cari told him. 'They're all dead, so there's no ongoing work for you.'

He glanced up at her sharply. 'Hey, Cari,' he smiled ruefully, 'I'm sorry—I didn't mean to complain. I gather you and Blair must have had one hell of a night.'

'Blair did. There wasn't a lot for me to do. As there's not a lot I can help him with now. These people don't want to see a doctor they've never met before. All I can do is the routine work, while he does the hard stuff.' She looked at the muddle of gear spread over the office. 'You take the morning to settle your gear back in,' she told him. 'I'll do the ward work before I go.'

'Before you go?' He sounded startled.

Cari nodded. 'The agreement was that I stay until you returned.'

'But as soon as this?'

'I'm no longer employed,' she said. 'Blair took me on because he was desperate. Now there's no reason for me to stay.'

'Are things that bad between you and Blair?' Rod demanded.

Cari was silent.

'Have you told him the truth about that negligence case yet?'

Her eyes flew to his face. 'I beg your pardon?'

'You know what I mean,' he said, his voice lowering. 'Is Blair still under the impression that you caused the kid's death?'

'I did,' Cari said firmly. 'I was found guilty in a court of law.'

Rod laughed shortly. 'Yeah, with who as witnesses?'

'I don't know what you're talking about.'

'Cari, you're mad! Why aren't you shouting your innocence from the rooftops instead of taking the rap for some elderly, incompetent anaesthetist who should have stopped practising years ago?'

All the colour had drained from Cari's face. She stared up at Rod and then sank down into the chair beside the desk.

'What did you hear?' she asked.

He stared down at her and shook his head disbelievingly. He shifted one of his bags from where he had tossed it on the other seat, and seated himself on the opposite side of the desk to her.

'My cousin's a surgeon at Chandler,' he said slowly, watching Cari's face as he talked. 'I think I've already told you, our families are close. He came over to visit my father, and I asked him to find out about you.'

Cari's eyes flew up to meet his. 'You had no business to,' she whispered.

'No,' he agreed. His boyish face broke into a smile. 'I'm just a born stickybeak. Anyway, he did, and I dropped in to see him on the way back here. What he told me doesn't quite fit with what you've told us, Cari.'

'I haven't told one lie. Not one,' she whispered fiercely.

'Yes, you have,' Rod said firmly. 'You said that your negligence caused the death of a child. It wasn't your negligence, was it, Cari?'

She was silent, staring at her hands.

'The way Ed heard it, the head of anaesthetics of Chandler Hospital is semi-retired. If he was anyone else he would have been pensioned off years ago, but he's married to a Chandler, a woman who controls much of the money backing the hospital. As a couple, they're rich, influential and have far too much say in the running of the hospital.'

Still Cari was silent. Rod sat back and studied her for a moment before continuing.

'When Ed started asking questions he found a whole lot of people who were feeling rotten about you, Cari. The story goes that the kid you were gassing came from one of California's more influential families. Is that right?'

She nodded mutely.

'And you were in charge, with things going well until

this semi-retired anaesthetist decided that it would look
better if he took over. So he came in and ordered you
off the job. And just after that he noticed that the
connection of the ventilator was loose and the child
was dying. He said it was as soon as he reached the
table. The story you initially told was that when you
handed the child over the connection was firm and the
child was fine.

'Only they didn't believe you, did they, Cari?' Rod
continued. 'The surgeon was in line for promotion.
The promotion was dependent on a board decision,
and that board consisted mainly of Chandlers. The
junior staff could be intimidated in much the same way
as I'd imagine you were intimidated. With no witnesses
on your side your story fell down in court, and finally
you were persuaded to accept the charge of negligence.
It was easier, in the long run, than to fight the stigma
of being branded a liar.'

'It still is,' said Cari.

Rod nodded. 'You're not a liar, though, Cari,' he
said firmly. 'And you're not negligent. Sure, within the
walls of the Chandler Hospital, no one can question
the court's ruling. But the staff, among themselves,
know what happened. And so does the medical community at large. They can't prove it, but they know.
Why else do you think you weren't struck off? You
didn't even get a reprimand from the medical board.'

She looked up, her eyes full of tears. 'Not just within
Chandler,' she said. 'My fiancé couldn't drop me fast
enough, and my father and brothers were so ashamed
they didn't want anything to do with me. When I said I
was coming to Australia, my father even warned me
not to try to practise again. He said. . . Well, it doesn't
matter. It's a long time ago now.' Her voice fell silent.

Rod stood and walked around to stand next to her.

'So why are you still running, Cari?' he asked gently. 'Why not stay here until you're back on your feet, until you've got some confidence back again?'

'And ease the work-load for you and Blair?' Cari smiled through her tears and Rod grinned, unabashed.

'There is that,' he agreed.

She shook her head and stood up, wiping away the tears impatiently with the back of her hand.

'No.' She dredged up a smile. 'Thank you for your faith, Rod, but I can't. I'm not ready for medicine again.'

'So what have you been doing for the last month?'

'Something I'd rather not have been doing.'

'You didn't enjoy it?' he demanded. He looked at her closely. 'Come on, Cari, admit it. Medicine is like a drug. You start it and it becomes a way of life. You can't just decide to become an encyclopaedia salesman instead. It doesn't work that way.'

'It doesn't matter. I can't stay here.'

Rod opened his eyes wide and stared at her, his mind suddenly finding another track.

'You're in love with Blair Kinnane, aren't you?'

'No.'

He stood back and eyed her speculatively. 'Cari Eliss, you make a lousy liar,' he said bluntly. 'Nothing else makes sense. I did wonder before I left, but. . . I'm right, aren't I?'

Cari was silent.

'So what you're running from is not medicine any more. It's personal involvement.'

She took a deep breath. 'You're wasted in general practice, Rod,' she told him. 'You'd make a great psychiatrist. Now, if you'll excuse me, I've got work to do before I go.'

'Does Blair love you?'

'That's none of your business.'

He eyed her speculatively. 'Why don't you give yourself a chance?' he suggested. 'I'll tell him what happened——'

'No!' The word came out sharp and hard. 'Look, Rod, I'm in a mess. I can't cope with personal entanglements. I've got my life in a mess, and I don't want to get anyone else involved.'

'It seems to me that Blair Kinnane is very well able to take care of himself,' Rod said drily.

'He's got enough on his plate without my problems,' Cari said bitterly. 'I don't want him feeling sorry for me. Rod, you're not to tell him.'

'You're crazy!' he expostulated.

'All right, I'm crazy,' she said firmly. 'Add it to the things that Cari Eliss is. The only thing that Cari Eliss definitely isn't any more is a doctor at Slatey Creek. I've got about a two-hour ward-round to do and then I'm finished. My debt to the Flying Doctor Service is paid in full and I'm leaving.' She walked out of the little office and slammed the door.

She did a thorough ward-round, getting as much work done as she could to leave the place in order for Blair and Rod. For the patients she had been treating herself she made meticulous notes, leaving nothing to chance.

She farewelled each of her patients sadly. She had gained a lot from her short time here. As she put the last chart back on the end of the bed, she grimaced to herself. Was this the end of her medical career? It had to be, she thought bleakly.

The hospital entrance was still crowded. Blair was nowhere to be seen.

It was cowardly to leave like this, Cari acknowledged to herself, but she couldn't do it any other way. To walk in on his office where he would be caught up with bereaved parents and announce that she was leaving was impossible.

She drove slowly back out to the Bromptons', aching with loss.

'So when are you going?' Maggie had her hands on her hips and was staring at Cari in dismay.

'Tomorrow morning at first light. I want to get as far as possible before I camp tomorrow night.'

'You're crazy!'

'Maggie, I can't stay here for ever.' Cari attempted a smile. 'Even you and Jock would get sick of me eventually. It's better that I go before my welcome wears thin.'

'It's better you wait until after the rain.'

Cari stared outside and frowned. The sky was already starting to show signs that Rod's prediction would be proved right. Along the horizon was a long, low cloud bank, slowly building up. It was the first dark cloud she had seen since her arrival.

'I've got the truck,' she said reassuringly. 'It can cope with bad weather.' She looked down at the little dog arching his back against her legs. 'And I've got Rusty.' She knew she should leave the little dog behind. It was by far the most sensible thing to do. He looked up at her as she stirred her foot to rub his soft belly and she knew she could do no such thing. She was beginning to wonder about quarantine regulations in the United States. She stooped and swung him up into her arms. Rusty was now her only link with this place, and she couldn't leave him.

'Does Blair know you're going?' Maggie demanded suddenly.

'The agreement was that I stay until Rod returned,' Cari told her.

'You haven't told him specifically that you're leaving tomorrow morning?'

'He was busy. I couldn't get near him.' Cari spread her hands helplessly. 'Look, Maggie, don't make this any harder for me. I have to go. I don't want to, but I have to. Can you just accept that?'

Before they could answer the back screen door swung open and Jock walked into the kitchen. He looked at the box of supplies Cari was packing on the kitchen table and frowned.

'You're not heading off into that?' He gestured to the blackening horizon.

'Yes, I am.' Cari was close to tears. 'Please, Jock, I'm really grateful to you and Maggie, but I'm not staying any longer. I need to go.'

'You'd be a damned fool if you did.'

'Why?' she demanded.

'What happens if we get floods?' Jock said harshly. 'This country's littered with dry creek beds. In the wet they can turn into rivers a kilometre across.'

Cari stared at him in amazement. 'It hasn't even started to rain yet! How do you know it's going to flood!'

'I didn't say it would. I just said that it might happen.'

'So when did you last get a flood?'

'Six years back,' Jock admitted.

'Well then,' Cari said with finality. She picked up her box of packed utensils and headed out to her near-ready truck, her little dog at her heels.

She went to bed early that night, in readiness for her early start. She lay and stared at the ceiling, willing sleep to come. As the sounds of the house signalled that Jock and Maggie too were starting to prepare for bed, the sound of the telephone shrilled through the house Cari bit her lip. She could guess who it would be.

'Cari?' It was Maggie's voice at the bedroom door. 'Cari, it's Blair on the phone.' Cari didn't answer. She turned her head into the pillow and closed her eyes.

'Cari?' Maggie's voice rose.

Cari buried her head further and willed Maggie to cease trying.

There was a long silence on the other side of the door. Finally there was the sound of Maggie's retreating footsteps and her voice as she picked up the phone in the hall.

'I'm sorry, Blair, but she's gone to bed early and I can't wake her.' The phone was put down. Maggie's footsteps returned to Cari's bedroom door.

'I hope you know what the hell you're doing,' her voice said softly through the door.

Cari turned over and stared at the darkened ceiling. She hoped she did too. She shook her head numbly in the dark and acknowledged the truth to herself. She didn't have a clue.

CHAPTER FOURTEEN

The Bromptons were all up to see Cari off the next morning. Cari ate a scant breakfast and threw the last of her belongings into the truck. These people had become her friends, and she hated to leave them. They stood on the veranda in the half-light of dawn and waved until their reflections faded to nothing in Cari's rear-vision mirror.

True to Jock's and Rod's predictions, it was raining. The rain was falling in a steady torrent. Rusty had become soaked before Cari had put him in the truck and his body was now steaming gently in the heat, filling the cabin with the odour of wet dog.

At least the rain in this country doesn't mean cold, Cari thought gratefully. She thought of her flimsy two-man tent and grimaced to herself. With luck the rain would have ceased before she pulled off the road to camp that evening. Otherwise she would be sleeping in the truck.

She had to pass through Slatey Creek to join the main road. The little settlement looked bedraggled and sodden, the main street already starting to turn from dust to mud.

She slowed as she passed through the settlement. As she neared the hospital she caught her breath. Blair's vehicle was parked on the verge, and it took only a momentary glance to tell her that Blair was at the wheel.

For a moment she contemplated putting her foot on the accelerator, but her foot wouldn't co-operate. The truck slowed further and she pulled in to park the truck in front of Blair's. She sat where she was and waited.

A moment later the passenger door swung open and Blair climbed in beside her. His large frame was protected from the rain by a generously-sized water-proof coat, down which rivulets of water ran to form a pool at his feet. Rusty attempted to growl a protest at being dislodged from his passenger-seat. Blair picked up the little dog and deposited him in the back of the truck.

'I don't think much of your guard dog, lady,' he told Cari, and Cari attempted a smile. She was shocked at Blair's appearance. He looked almost haggard.

'Have you had any sleep?' she asked him.

'Not much.'

She was silent. All she wanted to do was to take this man into her arms and smooth away the lines of fatigue. It was a Herculean task to hold herself rigid, to keep her hands on the steering wheel.

'How did you know I was leaving?' she asked.

'I rang the Bromptons five minutes ago. Maggie told me.'

Cari nodded.

'You weren't intending to say goodbye?' Blair asked dispassionately.

'I said goodbye,' Cari said defensively. 'When you were asleep.'

He nodded. 'That sounds like you,' he said grimly.

She was silent.

'Where are you going?' His tone was of polite enquiry.

'To Perth.'

'By which route?'

'It's none of your business.'

Blair took a deep breath. 'It is my business,' he said

wearily. 'Against solid advice you're heading off into the outback as we're getting the first decent rain we've had for years. This country doesn't absorb the water. It forms lakes and rivers where there've never been lakes and rivers.'

'It'll have stopped by tonight,' she insisted.

'If it has, well and good. What I want from you is the route that you intend taking and the first settlement that you intend travelling through.'

'You don't have to check up on me,' Cari said defensively.

'Don't I? Who else will?' Blair's voice was harsh with anger.

'No one. I've told you, I don't need anyone.'

He stared at her for a long moment, his anger not fading from his eyes. Then he reached for the box of maps on the seat beside her and pulled out the map of the area she intended travelling in. 'Show me,' he demanded.

Cari shrugged. 'I don't know myself yet.'

'Then make up your mind now,' he ordered. 'Otherwise I'll ring the local police and have you stopped by force. In this country you tell people where you're going. You tell them how long you're going to take to get there and you make sure there's a way they can check that you arrive.' He pointed to the settlement south-west of them on the map. 'Ridge Bark. Is that your next stop?'

'I suppose so,' Cari said doubtfully.

'Ridge Bark it is, then,' he said roughly. 'By tomorrow night. Call into the local police station when you get there and let them know you've arrived.'

'But that's crazy!'

'It's crazy not to.' He pointed to the tracks shown on the map. 'Show me your route.'

Five minutes later he was satisfied. He folded the map and put it away.

'OK, Cari.' His eyes were still cold and angry.

'Thank you for your concern,' she said quietly.

He laughed harshly. Turning in the cramped cabin, he gripped her shoulders. 'You could have had more than my concern if you'd had the courage,' he said grimly.

'Courage?'

'To trust. It's not that you believe I don't trust you, is it, Cari? It's that you can't trust me.'

Cari looked up into the deep grey eyes, full of hurt and anger, and her heart turned over in a spasm of love and desire.

'Oh, Blair,' she whispered. 'I wish I could turn the clock back and make me what I was.'

'I don't want what you were,' he said angrily, shaking her shoulders. 'It's the Cari Eliss that's in front of me now that I want. Only she can't find the courage to bury the past, to tell me about it and then get on with rebuilding her life. She hasn't got the guts.'

She looked up at him, tears blinding her. 'I'm sorry, Blair,' she whispered. 'I'm sorry.'

He stared down at her, then suddenly bent his head and kissed her, a hard, brutal, demanding kiss. When he finally released her, she could taste the salt of blood on her lip.

'I'm sorry too,' he said harshly. He released her shoulders and turned to climb from the truck. While Cari fumbled with the ignition and finally brought her truck back to life, he stood in the teeming rain and watched. As she rounded the curve leading away from town she looked back. He was still standing at the edge of the road.

*   *   *

Cari had never seen rain like it. It matched her mood. There was no need for her to cry while the heavens were performing the task for her.

When Blair had mentioned Ridge Bark as being two days' drive away her first reaction had been that she could be almost to Perth by then. By midday she was beginning to realise that Ridge Bark was an achievement in itself. The rain showed no sign of easing, and the dusty roads were fast becoming slippery, muddy quagmires. Her wheels churned and slid and it took all her concentration to keep the vehicle on the road.

Rusty nested himself comfortably beside her, his head trustingly laid in her lap. 'At least you think I know what I'm doing,' Cari muttered as she ventured a hand off the wheel to pat the little dog's head. Rusty stirred, sighed and settled again.

She slept that night in the truck. There was no way she could set the tent up without being soaked in the process, and she didn't like her chances of having dry bedding at the end of it. Her sleep was a fitful slumber, marred by cramps and the aches of her past injuries.

As the dark receded to show another rain-filled day Cari and Rusty ate dry biscuits and fruit and started off again. Cari was longing for coffee, but there was no room in the confines of the truck to heat the Primus, and outside was a steady sheet of rain.

As her second day of travel progressed the truck slowed to a crawl, and she looked at the map in concern. She had told Blair she would make Ridge Bark by tonight, but she was not halfway there.

Surely he would realise that the bad weather was delaying her? She didn't want his concern on top of everything else. She had caused him enough trouble, she thought bitterly.

She shut the thought of him from her mind. All she

could do was to keep on going, to stay rigidly to the tracks she had shown Blair and hope that this torrential rain would soon ease.

On her way in to Slatey Creek all those weeks ago Cari had crossed several dry creek beds, most of them clearly shown on the map and used as landmarks. Similar creeks were between Slatey Creek and Ridge Bark, but they were no longer dry.

Cari's truck forded three, one after another, each a shallow, swift rush of debris-laden water. The fourth one she only just managed to put the truck through, and her worry deepened. The next time she would have to check the water level and, if it was any deeper, she could not cross.

Ten minutes later she came across the next creek and knew that she had reached the end of this route for the truck.

This was no creek. It was a swirling mass of white water, three hundred metres wide. As she climbed from the truck to gaze in dismay, more and more of the land banking the newly formed river was disappearing under the onrush.

She had parked the truck five metres from the water's edge. She climbed back in and reversed swiftly, taking her vehicle to higher ground.

There wasn't much. This land was a flat plain, stretching forever.

Cari looked down at the map on the seat. The last small waterway she had sucessfully crossed seemed to be an offshoot of this main creek. To her dismay, on the map the watercourses appeared to form an enclosed loop. Within the loop there was no track leading off to either right or left.

Her only chance lay in doubling back, re-crossing the smaller creek and getting off this track. Remember-

ing the truck's labour at crossing the creek ten minutes
earlier, she bit her lip and gunned the truck into action.

She could go nowhere. In the twenty minutes it had
taken her to travel to and return from the main creek,
the smaller offshoot had swollen, bursting its shallow
banks to spill water out in foaming arcs in all directions.

Cari climbed out of the truck. Ignoring her light
sneakers and jeans, she waded out to the point where
the creek bed dropped away. At this point the water
was up to her knees. Ahead of her it fell, nearly
another metre. There was no way her truck could re-
cross.

Rusty whined as she climbed back into the truck. He
put his nose down and sniffed the soaked denim of her
jeans, then looked up in concern at her face.

'I know what you're thinking,' Cari said grimly. 'I've
been a fool.' She put her hand down and ran it lightly
over the little dog's coat, seeking reassurance in his
closeness. 'We're just going to have to follow the creek
around and see if we can find somewhere we can cross.'

There was nowhere. Within fifteen minutes Cari had
established that the track crossed the creek at the
shallowest points. Everywhere else was even more
threatening.

She drove the truck to the highest piece of ground.
'We're marooned,' she told Rusty grimly. 'We're surrounded by water.'

Rusty sighed deeply and put his head on her lap.

'I agree,' Cari said firmly. 'It's just awful.' She picked
the little dog up and put him on her lap. 'Any
suggestions?'

Rusty put a tongue up and reached to lick her face,
and she nodded. 'Do nothing and wait for the water to
go down?' she asked. 'I guess you're right.' She looked

out of the window and grinned ruefully. 'At least we're not going to be short of drinking water!'

They woke to more rain. After another cramped night with little sleep Cari opened her eyes to water, as far as the eye could see. She sat up and rubbed her eyes disbelievingly.

She had chosen the highest part of land within the loop to park the truck for the night. The enclosed loop at dusk the night before had been perhaps two kilometres wide, maybe even more. Now she could see the banks of both streams forming the loop. The width was perhaps three hundred metres, no more.

For the first time, Cari felt a prickle of fear crawl down the small of her back. She shifted Rusty, who was still sleeping comfortably, his head nestled across her legs. He looked up enquiringly.

'Rusty, boy, we may just be in trouble,' Cari said quietly.

He pricked his ears.

'Come on,' she told him. 'I'm going to have to have a look, and if I'm going to get soaked then I don't see why you shouldn't!'

It was a relief to get out of the cramped confines of the truck, even if both Cari and the dog were sodden two minutes after emerging. She walked the short distance to where the river started, and gazed in horror. The water was so wide that, in the driving rain, she could not make out the opposite bank. It would have to be shallow, she thought, at least most of the way across, but somewhere in its midst was the old creek bed, where it would fall away. It was a swirling mass of debris-laden water. There was no way she could possibly swim to the other side.

And the water was rising. She stood at the edge for

five minutes and in that time the water had swallowed another metre's width of dry land. She had to move back, and move back again.

'We should have abandoned the truck yesterday and crossed the creek while we still had the chance,' she whispered to herself. It was too late now. She put a hand down and held firmly on to Rusty's collar, seeking reassurance from his presence.

For fifteen minutes she stood watching. The water rose while she watched. She looked back at where the truck was standing, still high and dry. If the water continued rising at this rate, their little island would have disappeared before nightfall. Earlier.

And them with it. Cari had no doubt as to their fate if the swirling waters rose sufficiently to sweep the truck away. She shivered and stooped to take the little dog into her arms.

'Come on, Rusty,' she said, 'let's make some breakfast.'

The worst part was that there was nothing to do. Cari ate a desultory meal and fed Rusty. Then they sat on the bedding in the back of the truck and waited for the rain to stop.

It had no intention of stopping. It was as if someone had suddenly remembered that this barren centre hadn't been watered for years, and had turned on the tap, trying to make up in days for what this place had been deprived of for years. Cari watched the water slowly approach the higher ground and began to accept the inevitable.

All she could think of was Blair. Her rejection of Blair, which she had done with such high motives, suddenly seemed crazy, totally and absolutely insane. What had she been doing? She had driven away from him with resolution. She had faced that loss with the same empty desolation that she had accepted the end of her medical career. Now, when that loss seemed like being forever, and forever seemed so short, the thought of losing him was unbearable.

He had been right, she acknowledged to herself with awful clarity. She had been a coward. A coward meekly to throw in her medical career and a coward not to grasp at the chance of happiness with Blair. She had been knocked from her secure little pedestal, and she had been too afraid to climb back from her base for fear of being knocked again. Now it looked as if even the base was being taken from her.

'Oh, Blair,' she whispered, 'I'm sorry.' She looked down at Rusty. 'And I'm sorry for you too,' she told him. Suddenly the thought of the little dog being drowned was more than she could bear. She put her face down into the dog's soft fur and wept.

Rusty heard it first. His head was burrowed into her shoulder, but he pulled away and sat upright, ears cocked at their usual crazy angle. He whined, broke from Cari's hold and pawed at the door of the truck. It wasn't completely closed, and swung open. Rusty leapt out into the rain to stand looking skyward.

Cari stared after him, then her gaze swung skyward too as she heard what Rusty had heard. She climbed out of the truck. Above them was the drone of an aircraft, travelling low.

As they watched, the little plane broke from the low-lying cloud. Silver against the grey of the sky, its blue insignia could plainly be seen. The insignia of the Australian Flying Doctor Service.

It was Blair. Up there was Blair. Cari closed her eyes as tears continued to stream down her cheeks. He must have checked with Ridge Bark last night and discovered that she hadn't reached her destination.

Blair. The thought held her motionless, unmoving, as the aircraft made a low sweep overhead.

The plane made two passes before Cari pulled herself together. She suddenly realised what Blair, or whoever was piloting the plane, was trying to do. He would be trying to assess how stable the track was to land.

She pulled herself togther. She climbed back into the truck, Rusty following. Revving the engine, she drove the length of the track until it disappeared into the murky water, then she turned and drove in the other direction. Under the wheels of the truck the road was still reasonably solid. If the pilot had seen her driving he should have been able to assess that. Cari pulled the truck well off the track and waited. She looked fearfully along the road. The water was still eroding its length. Would he have enough room?

The plane came in. For a moment Cari thought it was going to land, and held her breath, but it simply roared in, flew low, then reared skyward.

It banked sharply, then came in again. Cari closed her eyes. When she opened them the plane was down.

For a moment she didn't move. She couldn't. Then the door to the cockpit was open and Blair was climbing down. Somehow the distance between them disappeared. Somehow Cari found herself in his arms, laughing and sobbing and holding him as if she could never let him go.

CHAPTER FIFTEEN

THERE was little time for talking on the flight back to Slatey Creek. Cari sat beside Blair in the cockpit, trying to come to terms with what had happened, while Blair concentrated on keeping the little plane on course.

They had moved swiftly. Blair had only just managed to pull the plane up short of the water. Together they managed to push it around to face the way it had come. Cari had grabbed her most precious belongings from the truck and the plane was sent hurtling down the track.

Neither of them had thought that the plane could possibly lift in such a short distance, but somehow it had. Now, safe for the time being before Blair had to attempt another landing at Slatey Creek, Cari had time to catch her breath and realise that, once again, life was stretching out before her.

She stole a look at Blair. His face was grim and drawn with concentration.

'I didn't know you flew,' she said tentatively, almost nervously. During the first embrace he had held her, sensing her desperate need for reassurance that he was real and not some fevered imagining of her terrified mind. Then there had been short, sharp instructions as they had prepared for the return flight. Now it was as if they were both afraid, as frightened of this emotion between them as they were of the physical dangers they were facing.

'I've got my licence,' he said brusquely. 'I normally

leave the flying to Luke, but I couldn't ask him to risk his neck out here.'

Cari was effectively silenced. She sat holding Rusty to her for comfort. The little dog was looking out of the cockpit window with dismay. The ground seemed an awfully long way down for one small dog. He whimpered, and she held him closer.

The radio crackled into life and Cari recognised Luke's anxious voice.

'Blair?'

Blair acknowledged. In a few short words he told Luke what had happened.

'I've been on to Ridge Bark,' Luke said. 'If anything, conditions are worse there than they are here. This strip's a quagmire, though.'

'It can't be any worse than we've already experienced.' Blair threw a tired smile to Cari. 'Cross your fingers for us, Luke. We're coming home!'

Slatey Creek was almost totally shrouded in low-lying cloud. It was just as well this country wasn't mountainous, Cari thought, or they would never have been able to find their way back. Blair stayed low, following the faint lines of the tracks, below them water was everywhere.

'You'll be cut off for months at this rate,' Cari said in amazement, but Blair shook his head.

'The inland lakes have been dry for years now,' he said. 'If this rate of rainfall keeps up most of this water will find its way into them. Slatey Creek will start seeing waterbirds again.'

Cari shook her head in disbelief. 'I'd like to see it.'

'I hope you will,' he said curtly. His attention was riveted on the faint outline of the runway, dead ahead. 'Hold on to your hat, Cari. We're going down.'

Until they landed Cari had not fully appreciated the

risks that Blair was running. The wheels touched down, and she let her breath out in a long sigh of relief. As she did the wheels lost their grip in the sodden sand, and the little plane veered wildly and spun.

It didn't crash. Somehow, miraculously, it stayed upright and came to rest halfway down the runway, facing back the way it had come. Blair cut the ignition and closed his eyes.

If Cari could have found a hole, deep and dark and all-enveloping, she would have cheerfully crawled into it. As it was, she faced Luke and the other anxious people who had gathered at the airport.

Jock was there. He removed a very relieved Rusty from her grasp before enveloping her in a bear-hug. 'Next time you'll take the advice of your betters, girl,' he growled, and Cari nodded shamefacedly.

'I'm sorry to worry you all,' she said quietly.

'Well, you couldn't have known it'd keep up like this,' Jock said cheerfully. 'If I'd have guessed I'd have locked you in your bedroom and swallowed the key.' He grinned. 'Just don't make me be the one who has to ring your insurance company about the truck!' Obviously the people waiting had listened to Blair's radio conversation with Luke.

Cari's eyes widened in dismay. 'I suppose there's no hope it will be still there when the water goes down?' she asked hesitantly,

'The water's still rising,' Jock said firmly. 'And I dare say when the water drops your truck will be somewhere, but it sure as heck won't be where you left it. Now, can I drive you back out to our place?'

Blair's voice cut in from where he had been talking to Luke. 'Cari's coming with me,' he said. He managed a grin. 'I'd appreciate it if you took the Animal, though.'

Jock raised his eyebrows. 'OK with you, Cari?'

'I. . .' Cari took a deep breath and looked over to the haggard face of the man she loved. 'Yes,' she said softly.

Ten minutes later they swung in to the hospital entrance. Blair walked around to the passenger door and stood as Cari climbed down from the truck.

'Hot showers all round, I think,' he said and Cari looked up to meet his eyes.

He still loved her. Whatever she had done to destroy his faith in her, this man loved her. It was written in the way his eyes rested on her face. Tears filled her eyes, and she put a hand out to lightly touch his soaked shoulder.

'Blair. . .'

'Blair!' It was a shout from the doorway. Rod was standing under the canopy of the hospital entrance. Their gaze broke and they turned.

'I'm sorry,' Rod called to them. 'I've got an appendix here that needs urgent attention. Can you help?'

Blair sighed and started forward, but Cari caught his arm.

'Blair, I'll do it,' she said firmly. 'You're exhausted. Go and have a shower.'

He frowned.

'Go on,' she insisted. 'I've had nothing to do in that damned truck except sleep, while you've been working and worrying and piloting planes in awful conditions. Go on.' They had reached the steps where Rod was standing. She looked up at Rod in appeal. 'Do you want an exhausted, wrung-out anaesthetist or a nice young, fresh-faced, enthusiastic and competent anaesthetist who's raring to go?'

Rod laughed and spread his hands. 'What can I say to that?' he asked Blair, and Blair smiled wearily.

'Competent anaesthetist?' he asked Cari.

'Competent anaesthetist,' Cari said firmly. Blair nodded.

'As soon as you left, Rod decided that his promise was no longer binding and told me everything,' he told her. 'You've been bloody stupid.'

'I know, I know.' She met his gaze openly. 'I think I've been a fool in more ways than one.'

There was a long silence. Rod's gaze went from one to the other. Finally he cleared his throat.

'I've still got a child in here who needs someone to put her to sleep,' he said, laughter in his voice. 'If one of you could decide—or perhaps you could do it holding hands?'

Cari laughed. The sound caught her by surprise. She sounded young, she thought joyfully. Young and gloriously free.

'Go on,' she told Blair firmly. 'Go and get into a shower. I'll cope with this. I'll come and find you when I've finished.'

'You won't run away again?'

She looked expressively up at the heavens. 'You see me trapped in circumstances beyond my control, Dr Kinnane.' She smiled. The answering smile in his eyes made her heart leap within her. She took a breath and turned away. 'Let's get rid of one appendix,' she told Rod.

The appendix was messy. It was over an hour before Cari could leave the theatre and make her way back to Blair's apartment. She knocked at his door. When there was no answer she opened the door silently and went in.

He was asleep. He had showered, pulled on a pair
of light trousers and lain on the bed to wait for her. A
book lay beside him, dropped on to the floor as sleep
had overtaken him.

Cari came forward and looked down into the beloved
face. In sleep the harsh lines of exhaustion had disappeared and he looked young and vulnerable.

She left him sleeping. She showered, taking a long
time to soak the accumulated grime of the past three
days from her body. She had scrubbed swiftly for
Theatre and her hands were scrupulously clean. The
rest had been covered with theatre garb and, surveying
herself ruefully in the bathroom mirror, she acknowledged that it left a lot to be desired in the cleanliness
stakes. She soaped herself from head to toe, then
soaped herself again.

Finally she emerged, pink with glowing cleanliness.
She used one of Blair's thick white towels to dry
herself, then wrapped herself in another and made her
way back to the bedroom. She sat beside the sleeping
Blair, towelling her damp hair and watching the steady
rhythm of his breathing.

Finally she ran a comb through her near-dry hair,
looked down lovingly at the sleeping man and slid
under the covers at his side. She placed her arms lightly
around him. He stirred slightly in his sleep but didn't
wake. For a few moments Cari lay wakeful, savouring
the feel of this man beside her. Then she too was
overtaken by sleep.

They woke as darkness was starting to settle over
the room. Blair stirred first and Cari's eyes opened.
Her body moved languorously against his and he
turned.

'How long have you been here?' His voice was slurred with sleep.

'Hours and hours,' she said teasingly.

'Hours and hours?' Blair moved to look at the clock near the bed. 'Good God,' he said. He propped himself up on an elbow and looked down at her. 'Did the appendix go all right?'

'Just fine, Dr Kinnane.'

He nodded. 'I wouldn't expect anything else from my competent medical staff,' he said firmly.

'Am I employed again?' asked Cari.

He put a finger down and lightly touched her nose. 'As I seem to recall, Dr Eliss, I've pulled you from a very dicey situation not once but twice. Two times, Dr Eliss.'

'So?' she said cautiously.

'So, once again you're indebted to the Flying Doctor Service. And this time I intend to exact my payment in full.'

She looked up at him, her eyes full of love and laughter.

'By putting me to work?'

He nodded. 'From dawn to dusk,' he promised. 'And after dusk I have other plans.'

'Which are?'

'Indescribable,' he said calmly. 'I'm just going to have to demonstrate.'

For a long moment they stayed, searching each other's eyes. Then Blair pulled back the soft cotton covers and gathered her body into him.

Afterwards they lay quiet, warm with love but not yet ready for sleep. Blair's arm held Cari tightly against him, as if not willing to let her move a centimetre from his side.

'You'll marry me, Cari.'

She smiled and moved to kiss him softly on the lips. 'Is that a proposal or an order?'

'Both. Just say "Yes, sir".'

She pretended to consider. 'Is Rusty included in the contract?'

He groaned, but his eyes were filled with laughter. 'You drive a hard bargain, my lovely Cari. For you, however, I will even incorporate that disreputable mutt into my household. And if that's not a declaration of absolute devotion I don't know what is. Now, Dr Eliss, if you have no more clauses to include in the agreement, just close your eyes, and say "Yes, sir".'

Cari closed her eyes. 'Yes, sir.' She sighed, a long-drawn-out sigh of pure contentment. 'Blair?'

'Yes, my love?'

'Love me.'

He pulled her down so that her hair fell on to his chest. He stroked the smooth skin of her back, running his fingers lightly over the curve of her spine. Her body moved of its own accord, stirring with arousal.

He found her face and kissed her, gently at first and then deeply, demandingly. Then he broke away, looking up into her love-filled eyes.

'Did you say, "Love me"?' he murmured.

'Yes.' It was a whisper.

'For how long?'

'How long can you manage?' she asked shakily.

He cupped her face between his hands. His body moved to possess her, utterly.

'I'm not sure,' he responded softly, as their bodies joined and merged in a glory of love, of trust and desire. 'How long is forever?'

4 MEDICAL ROMANCES
AND 2 FREE GIFTS
From Mills & Boon

Capture all the excitement, intrigue and emotion of the busy medical world by accepting four FREE Medical Romances, plus a FREE cuddly teddy and special mystery gift. Then if you choose, go on to enjoy 4 more exciting Medical Romances every month! Send the coupon below at once to:

MILLS & BOON READER SERVICE, FREEPOST PO BOX 236, CROYDON, SURREY CR9 9EL.
No stamp required

- - - ✂ - - - - - - - - - - - - - - - - - - ✂ - - -

YES! Please rush me my 4 Free Medical Romances and 2 Free Gifts! Please also reserve me a Reader Service Subscription. If I decide to subscribe, I can look forward to receiving 4 Medical Romances every month for just £6.40, delivered direct to my door. Post and packing is free, and there's a free Mills & Boon Newsletter. If I choose not to subscribe I shall write to you within 10 days - I can keep the books and gifts whatever I decide. I can cancel or suspend my subscription at any time. I am over 18.

EP19D

Name (Mr/Mrs/Ms) _____

Address _____

_____

_____ Postcode _____

Signature _____

— MEDICAL ♥ ROMANCE —

The books for enjoyment this month are:

CAUGHT IN THE CROSSFIRE Sara Burton
PRACTICE MAKES PERFECT Caroline Anderson
WINGS OF HEALING Marion Lennox
YESTERDAY'S MEMORY Patricia Robertson

♥   ♥   ♥   ♥   ♥

Treats in store!

Watch next month for the following absorbing stories:

DEMPSEY'S DILEMMA Christine Adams
WIND OF CHANGE Clare Lavenham
DOCTOR ON SKYE Margaret O'Neill
CROSSROADS OF THE HEART Judith Worthy